Join the Club!

Be part of something special!

The Babysitters Club

Mary Anne Saves the Day

Ann M. Martin

SCHOLASTIC

Scholastic Children's Books
An imprint of Scholastic Ltd
Euston House, 24 Eversholt Street
London, NW1 1DB, UK
Registered office: Westfield Road, Southam, Warwickshire, CV47 0RA
SCHOLASTIC and associated logos are trademarks and/or registered
trademarks of Scholastic Inc.

First published in the US by Scholastic Inc, 1987
First published in the UK by Scholastic Ltd, 1988

This edition published in the UK by Scholastic Ltd, 2010

ISBN 978 1407 12041 6

A CIP catalogue record for this book is available from
the British Library.

Printed in the UK by CPI Bookmarque, Croydon, Surrey.
Papers used by Scholastic Children's Books are made from wood
grown in sustainable forests.

1 3 5 7 9 10 8 6 4 2

This book is for the real Claire and Margo,
Claire DuBois Gordon and Margo Méndez-Peñate,
Class of 2006.

Chapter 1

"Kristy! Hey, Kristy!" I called.

It was Monday afternoon, almost five-thirty, and time for a meeting of the Babysitters Club. I had just stepped on to my front porch. At the house next door, I could see Kristy Thomas stepping on to her front porch.

Kristy is the president of the Babysitters Club. She's also my best friend in the whole world. We've grown up together. And since my mother died when I was really little, leaving just Dad and me, Kristy's been like my sister, and Mrs Thomas is like my mother. (Kristy's parents got divorced a few years ago and her dad walked out, but my father has *not* been like a father to Kristy. He's not warm and open like Mrs Thomas.)

"Hi, Mary Anne," Kristy answered.

We ran across our front lawns, crunching through the remains of a January snow, and met between our houses. Then we crossed the

1

street to Claudia Kishi's house. Claudia is the vice president of the club. We hold our meetings at her house because she has a telephone in her bedroom.

The Babysitters Club is really more of a business than a club. This is how it works: on Monday, Wednesday and Friday afternoons, the club meets from five-thirty until six o'clock. Our clients call us on Claudia's line to tell us when they'll need babysitters. Then one of us takes the job. It's simple – but brilliant. (It was Kristy's idea.) The great thing is that with four of us taking the calls, anyone who needs a sitter is bound to find one.

Of course, our club isn't perfect. For instance, the members – Kristy, Claudia, me (I'm the secretary) and Stacey McGill, who's our treasurer – are only twelve years old. The latest we can stay out is ten o'clock. In fact, only Stacey is actually allowed out that late, although recently sometimes Claudia has been allowed to sit until ten, too. Kristy and I have to be home by nine-thirty on the weekends, and nine o'clock on weeknights. That nearly cost us our club. Recently, another bunch of girls copied us and set up a business called the Babysitters Agency. They were older than us and could stay out until all hours. A lot of our clients started using them instead, but the agency folded because the kids who worked for it weren't great babysitters, so now we're back to normal, glad that the new year is starting off smoothly.

Kristy rang the Kishis' bell, and Mimi answered the door. Mimi is Claudia's grandmother. She lives with the Kishis and watches out for Claudia and her sister, Janine, since both Mr and Mrs Kishi work.

"Hello, girls," said Mimi in her pleasant voice. The Kishis are Japanese. Claudia and Janine were born in the United States. Both of their parents came to America when they were little. Mimi was in her thirties, I think, when she left Japan, so she still speaks with an accent. I like her accent. It's soft and nice to listen to.

"Hi, Mimi," we replied.

"How is the scarf coming, Mary Anne?" she asked. (Mimi taught me how to knit. She's helping me make a scarf for my father.)

"It's fine," I said. "I'm almost done, but I'll need you to help me with the fringe."

"Of course. Any time, Mary Anne."

I kissed Mimi quickly on the cheek. Then Kristy and I got prepared to run up the stairs and into Claudia's room. We have to do it fast.

If Janine is home, we like to try to get by her bedroom without having to talk to her.

Janine is a genius. Honest. She's only fifteen and already she's taking classes at Stoneybrook University. She corrects absolutely everything you say to her. Kristy and I avoid her as much as possible.

That day, we were lucky. Janine wasn't even home. When we ran by her room, it was dark.

"Hi!" we greeted Claudia.

"Hi," she replied, her voice muffled. Claudia had her head in her pyjama bag as she rummaged around at the bottom of it. In a moment she straightened up, proudly holding out three Ring Dings.

Claudia is a junk-food addict. She buys candy and Twinkies and Wagon Wheels and other things and hides the stuff all over her room. She eats it at any time (and eats her meals, too) and never seems to gain an ounce, or to get so much as the hint of a pimple.

She handed us each a Ring Ding, but I turned mine down. Dad gets upset if I don't eat a proper dinner (or breakfast or lunch), and I don't have a very big appetite. Claudia tossed the Ring Ding back in her pyjama bag. She wasn't going to offer it to Stacey when she arrived, since Stacey has diabetes and can't eat most sweets.

4

"Any calls yet?" I asked. It was just barely five-thirty, but sometimes our clients called early.

"One," replied Claudia. "Kristy's mom. She needs someone for David Michael on Thursday."

Kristy nodded. "Our regular two-day-a-week sitter finally quit. Mom'll be calling more often for a while."

Kristy has two brothers in high school, Sam and Charlie, and a little brother, David Michael, who's six. Sam, Charlie and Kristy are each responsible for David Michael one afternoon a week. Mrs Thomas had had a babysitter lined up for him for the other two days, but I knew the sitter had been cancelling a lot.

"Hey, everybody!" called a voice. Stacey entered Claudia's room, looking gorgeous, as usual.

If you ask Stacey, she'll tell you she's plain, but that's crazy. Stacey is glamorous. She moved to Stoneybrook, Connecticut, from New York City last summer. She's very sophisticated, and is even allowed to have her hair professionally styled, so that she has this fabulous-looking shaggy blonde mane, and she wears the neatest clothes – big, baggy shirts and tight-fitting jeans – and amazing jewellery, like parrots and palm trees. She even has a pair of earrings that consist of a dog for one ear and a bone for the other ear.

5

I'd give anything to be Stacey. Not to have diabetes, of course, but to have lived in New York City and to be able to dress up like a model every day. My father lets me dress like a model, too – a model of a six-year-old. I have to wear my hair in plaits (that's a *rule*), and he has to approve my outfit every day, which is sort of silly since he buys all my clothes. And what he buys are corduroy skirts and plain sweaters and blouses and penny loafers.

Just once, I'd like to go to school wearing skintight turquoise trousers, Stacey's "island" shirt with the flamingos and toucans all over it, and maybe bright red, high-top trainers. I'd like to create a sensation. (Well, half of me would. The other half would be too shy to want to attract any attention.)

Stacey often creates a sensation.

So does Claudia. Although she's not quite as sophisticated as Stacey (you can't top having lived in New York), she's pretty glamorous herself. Her black hair is long and silky, and she does something different with it almost every day. Sometimes she wears it in lots of skinny plaits; sometimes she twists it on top of her head. At the moment, she was wearing it loose, but had pulled the sides back with big yellow clips shaped like flowers.

Luckily, Kristy dresses more like me than like Claudia and Stacey. It's nice to have someone to feel babyish with. Mrs Thomas doesn't put any dressing restrictions on Kristy; it's just that Kristy doesn't care much about her appearance. Her brown hair is usually sort of messy, and she wears clothes only because it's against the law to go to school naked.

"What's going on?" asked Stacey.

"One call so far," replied Kristy. "My mom needs someone for David Michael on Thursday afternoon."

I opened our record book. The Babysitters Club keeps two books: the record book and a notebook. The record book is just what it sounds like – a book in which we keep our club records. Not only does it have our babysitting appointments, it has the addresses and phone numbers of our clients, and records of things like what rates our clients pay, how much each of us earns at each job, and which of us has paid our club dues. Stacey keeps track of anything to do with money and numbers.

The Babysitters Club Notebook is more like a diary. Kristy asked us to write up what happens at every job we go to. This is important because then the rest of us learn about our clients' problems, habits and special needs. For instance, after Claudia babysat for Eleanor and Nina Marshall the first time, she wrote up the job and mentioned that Nina is allergic to strawberries. Since we all have to read the notebook entries, it wasn't long before the whole club knew never to give Nina a strawberry.

As you can see, our club is well run and well organized. We have Kristy to thank for that, even if she *is* bossy sometimes (well, a lot of the time).

I turned to the appointment section of the record book. "Let's see," I said. "Thursday . . . Claudia, you're the only one free. Do you want to sit for David Michael?"

"Sure," she answered.

I entered the job information in the book, and Claudia called Mrs Thomas back at her office to tell her who the sitter would be.

As soon as she hung up, the phone rang.

Claudia answered it, since her hand was still on the receiver. "Hello, the Babysitters Club. . . Yes? . . . Oh, hi. . . Saturday afternoon? I'll check and call you right back. . . OK. Bye."

I had already turned the pages of the record book to Saturday.

"That was Watson, Kristy. He needs someone for about two hours on Saturday, from two till four."

Watson is Kristy's mother's fiancé. They plan to get married in the fall. Watson's divorced, just like Mrs Thomas, and has two little kids: Karen, who's five, and Andrew, who's three. They stay with him every other weekend. When Watson becomes Kristy's stepfather, Karen and Andrew will become her stepsister and stepbrother.

Even though Kristy loves Karen and Andrew and would want the job on Saturday, our club rule is to offer each job to everybody. "Well," I said, "it looks like nobody is babysitting on Saturday so far."

"No," said Stacey, "but I have a doctor's appointment."

"And Mimi's taking me shopping then," said Claudia.

"Well, that leaves you and me," I told Kristy. "You can have the job. I know you want to see Karen and Andrew."

"Thanks!" replied Kristy happily.

I was being nice, but I was also being chicken. There's this weird old woman, Mrs Porter, who lives next door to Watson. Karen says she's a witch and that her name is really Morbidda Destiny. She's very frightened of her. So am I. I didn't mind passing up the job.

Claudia called Watson back.

The phone rang two more times, and we set up two more jobs.

The next time it rang, Kristy answered it. "Hello, the Babysitters Club. . . Hi, Mrs Newton!"

Mrs Newton is one of our favourite clients. She has an adorable little boy named Jamie . . . and a new baby! Lucy wasn't even two months old. Mrs Newton didn't let us sit for Lucy very often, so a call from her was pretty exciting.

Claudia and Stacey and I listened eagerly to Kristy's end of the conversation, wondering if Mrs Newton needed a sitter just for Jamie or for Lucy, too. Each of us was hoping for a chance to take care of the new baby.

"Yes," Kristy was saying. "Yes. . . Oh, Jamie *and* Lucy." (Claudia and Stacey and I squealed with delight.) "Friday . . . six till eight. . . Of course. I'll be there. Great. See you." She hung up.

Kristy would be there?! What happened to offering jobs around? Claud and Stacey and I stared at each other. I don't know what my face looked like, but I could see a mixture of horror and anger on the others' faces.

Kristy, however, was beaming. She was so thrilled at the possibility of taking care of Lucy that at first she didn't even realize what she'd done.

10

"The Newtons are giving a cocktail party on Friday, and they need someone to watch the kids while they're busy with the guests," she explained. "I'm so excited! Six till eight . . . I'll probably get to give Lucy a bottle—" Kristy broke off, finally realizing that nobody else looked nearly as happy as she did. "Oh," she said. "Sorry."

"*Kristy!*" exclaimed Claudia. "You're supposed to offer the job around. You know that. It's *your* rule. I'd like to sit for Lucy, too."

"So would I," added Stacey.

"Me, too." I checked our record book. "And we're all free then."

"Boy," said Claudia sullenly. She produced a large piece of chewing gum from under the quilt on her bed, unwrapped it, popped it in her mouth and chewed away. "Some people around here sure are job-hogs."

"I *said* I was sorry," exclaimed Kristy. "Besides, look who's talking."

Uh-oh, I thought. This doesn't sound good.

"What do you mean, look who's talking?" said Claudia.

"Well," Stacey began, and I could tell that she was trying to be polite, "you *have* done that a lot yourself. Remember that job with Charlotte Johanssen? And the one with the Marshalls?"

"And the one with the Pikes?" I added cautiously. It was true. Claudia had forgotten to offer a lot of jobs.

"Hey, what are you guys? Elephants? Don't you ever forget anything?"

"Well, it *has* been a problem," said Kristy.

"I don't believe this!" cried Claudia. "*You*" (she pointed accusingly at Kristy) "break one of our rules, and everyone jumps on *me*! I didn't do anything. I'm innocent."

"*This* time," muttered Stacey.

"Hey," said Claudia. "If you're so desperate to have new friends here in Stoneybrook, don't argue with the ones you've got."

"Is that a threat?" exclaimed Stacey. "Because if it is, I don't need you guys. Don't forget where I'm from."

"We *know*, we *know* – New York. It's all you talk about."

"I was *going* to say," Stacey went on haughtily, "before I was interrupted, that I'm tough. And I'm a fighter, and I don't need anybody. Not stuck-up job-hogs" (she looked at Claudia) "or bossy know-it-alls" (Kristy) "or shy little babies." Me.

"I am not a shy little baby!" I said, but as soon as I said it, my chin began to tremble and my eyes filled with tears.

"Oh, shut up," Kristy said crossly. Sometimes she has very little patience with me.

But I'd had it. I jumped to my feet. "No, *you* shut up," I shouted at Kristy. "And you, too," I said to Stacey. "I don't care how tough you are or how special you think you are because of your dumb diabetes, you have no right—"

"Don't call Stacey's diabetes dumb!" Claudia cut in.

"And don't bother to stick up for me," Stacey shouted back at Claudia. "Don't do me any favours."

"No problem," Claudia replied icily.

"Hey," said Kristy suddenly. "Who were you calling a bossy know-it-all before?"

"Who do you think?" replied Stacey.

"*Me?!*" Kristy glanced at me.

"Don't tell me to shut up and then expect me to help you," I told Kristy.

Kristy looked as if someone had just informed her that scientists had discovered that the moon was in fact made of green cheese.

"Maybe I am shy," I said loudly, edging towards the door. "And maybe I am quiet, but you guys can*not* step all over me. You want to know what I think? I think you, Stacey, are a conceited snob; and you, Claudia, are a stuck-up job-hog; and you, Kristin Amanda Thomas, are the biggest, bossiest know-it-all in the world, and I don't care if I never see you again!"

I let myself out of Claudia's room, slamming the door behind me so hard that the walls shook. Then I ran down the stairs. Behind me, I could hear Claudia, Stacey and Kristy yelling at one another. As I reached the Kishis' front hall, Claudia's door slammed again. Two more pairs of feet thundered down the stairs.

I ran home, half hoping that either Kristy or Stacey would call after me. But neither one did.

Chapter 2

The last thing I wanted to do after our big fight was eat dinner with Dad, but he expects us to have a proper meal in the evening. Sometimes he fixes it, sometimes I do, but we always sit down in the kitchen and eat dinner at six-thirty.

Luckily, Dad was still at work when I got home from Claudia's that night. I was crying, and in no mood to speak to anybody. I slammed angrily around the kitchen. I took a pan of leftover pot roast out of the refrigerator, slammed the fridge shut, stuck the pan in the oven and slammed the oven shut. Then I got out plates and glasses, knives and forks, and slammed two cabinets and a drawer. I banged the things down on the table one at a time. Eight bangs.

Then I went upstairs to wash my face. By the time Dad got home, I looked a lot better and felt a little better.

"Mary Anne?" he called.

"Coming," I answered. I headed down the stairs, my hair neatly combed, my blouse tucked carefully into my skirt. Dad says it's important to look nice at mealtime.

"Hi," I said.

"Hello, Mary Anne." He leaned over so I could kiss his cheek. "Is dinner started?"

"Yes." (Dad hates when people say *yeah*. He also hates *shut up*, *hey*, *gross*, *stupid*, and a long list of other words that creep into my vocabulary whenever I'm not around him.) "I'm heating up the pot roast."

"That's fine," said Dad. "Let's just toss a salad. That will make a nice dinner."

Dad and I got out lettuce, tomatoes, a cucumber and some carrots. We chopped and tossed silently. In no time, a crisp salad was sitting in a glass bowl in the centre of the kitchen table. My father took the pot roast out of the oven and served up two portions.

We sat down and bowed our heads while Dad said grace. At the end, just before the "Amen", he asked God to watch over Alma. (Alma is my mother.) He does that before every meal, as far as I know, and sometimes I think he overdoes things. After all, my mother has been dead for almost eleven years. I bless her at night before I go to sleep, and it seems to me that that ought to be enough.

"Well, how was your day, Mary Anne?"

"Fine," I replied.

"How did you do on your spelling test?"

I took a bite of salad, even though I wasn't a bit hungry. "Fine. I got a ninety-nine. It was—"

"Mary Anne, *please* don't speak with your mouth full."

I swallowed. "I got a ninety-nine," I repeated. "It was the highest grade in the class."

"That's wonderful. I'm very proud of you. Your studying paid off."

I nodded.

"Did you have a meeting of your club this afternoon?" he asked.

"Yeah . . . *yes.*"

Kristy, Claudia and Stacey are all surprised that Dad allows me to be in the club and to do so much babysitting. What they don't know is that the only reason he likes our business is that he thinks it teaches me responsibility and how to plan ahead, save money, and that sort of thing.

"What went on? Anything special?" Dad attempted a smile.

I shook my head. There was no way I was going to tell him about the fight we'd had.

"Well," said Dad, trying hard to make conversation, "my case went . . . went very well today. Quite smoothly, really. I feel certain that we're going to win."

I shifted uncomfortably in my seat. I didn't know what case he was talking about, but I had a feeling I *should* have known. He'd probably told me about it. "That's great, Dad."

"Yes. Thank you."

We ate in silence for several minutes.

"This case is interesting because it demonstrates the extreme importance of honesty in business dealings," he said finally. "Always remember that, Mary Anne. Be scrupulously honest and fair. It will serve you in good stead."

"All right, Dad."

We ate in silence again, and it dawned on me that Dad and I sat across from each other at that table twice a day each weekday and three times a day on the weekends. If a meal averaged half an hour, that meant we spent over four hundred hours a year eating together, trying to make conversation – and we barely knew what to say to each other. He might as well have been a stranger I just happened to share food with sixteen times a week.

I pushed my pot roast around my plate.

"You're not eating, Mary Anne," my father said. "Are you feeling all right?"

"Yes, fine."

"Are you sure? You weren't filling up on snacks at the Kishis', were you?"

"No, Dad, I sw – I promise. I guess I'm just not very hungry."

"Well, try to eat your vegetables, at least. Then you may start your homework."

Dad made starting my homework sound like some kind of reward.

I forced down as much as I could manage. Then my father turned the radio on and listened to classical music while we cleaned up the kitchen. At last, I escaped to my bedroom.

I sat down at my desk and opened my maths book. A clean sheet of paper lay before me, along with two sharpened pencils and a pink rubber. But I couldn't concentrate. Before I had made so much as a mark on the paper, I got up and flopped down on my bed.

I remembered calling my friends: a conceited snob; a stuck-up job-hog; and the biggest, bossiest know-it-all in the world. I sincerely wished I hadn't said those things.

Then I remembered being called a baby and being told to shut up. I sincerely wished

Stacey and Kristy hadn't said *those* things.

I wished I could talk to somebody. Maybe I could phone Claudia. The only thing *she'd* said that afternoon was for me not to call Stacey's diabetes dumb, which really wasn't mean. But I am not allowed to use the phone after dinner unless I'm discussing homework.

I could ask my father for special permission to use the phone for non-homework business, but he'd want to know what that business was.

I sighed.

I glanced out of my window. The side window of my bedroom looks right into the side window of Kristy's bedroom next door. Her light was off, the room dark.

I sat cross-legged on my bed and gazed around. No wonder Stacey had called me a baby. My room looks like a nursery. There's no crib or changing table, but basically the room hasn't changed since I was three. It's decorated in pink and white, which my father had just naturally assumed every little girl would like. The truth is, I like yellow and navy blue. Pink is one of my least favourite colours.

The curtains, which are ruffly, are made of pink flowered fabric and are tied back with pink ribbons. The bedspread matches the curtains. The rug is pale pink shag, and the walls are white, with pink baseboards.

Living in my room is like living inside a cotton-candy machine.

What bothers me most, though, is what's on the walls – or rather, what isn't on them. I've spent a lot of time in Kristy's and Claudia's rooms, and I've been in Stacey's room twice, and I've decided that you can tell a lot about the people who use those rooms just by looking at the walls. For example, Kristy loves sports, so her walls are covered with posters about the Olympics and pictures of gymnasts and football players. Claudia is an artist and her own work hangs everywhere. She changes it often, taking down old paintings or drawings and putting up new ones. And Stacey, who misses New York more than she'll admit, has tacked up a poster of the city at night, another of the Empire State Building, and a map of Manhattan.

Here's what're on my walls: a framed picture of my parents and me, taken the day I was christened; a framed picture of Humpty Dumpty (before he broke); and two framed pictures of characters from *Alice in Wonderland*. They are all framed in pink.

Do you know what I would *like* to have on

my walls? I've thought about this very carefully, just in case my father should ever lose his mind and say I can redecorate. I'm not allowed to put up posters because the thumbtacks would make too many holes in the wall. But assuming Dad was really bonkers and didn't care about holes, I'd put up a giant poster of a kitten or maybe several kittens, a big photo of the members of the Babysitters Club, a poster of New York City, and maybe one of Paris.

I would take down Humpty and Alice, but leave the picture of my family.

My gaze drifted from my walls to the window. I snapped to attention as a light went on in Kristy's room. Maybe I could wave to her and let her know that as far as I was concerned, the fight was over. But Kristy pulled her shade down quickly, not even looking out of the window.

I checked my watch. It was almost eight o'clock. In another hour, I could try signalling to her with my torch. I worked out a torch code so that we can "talk" at night without the telephone. One of us usually flashes to the other shortly after nine o'clock. At that time, my father has already said goodnight to me. I'm free to read in bed until nine-thirty, but I know he won't check on me. Kristy and I have been signalling to each other for a long time and we have never been caught.

I finished my homework and changed into my nightgown. By five minutes to nine I was in bed, reading a very exciting book called *A Wrinkle in Time*.

Dad stuck his head in the door. "Oh, good. I see you're all ready for bed."

I nodded.

"What are you reading?"

"*A Wrinkle in Time*. It's on Mr Counts's reading list." (Mr Counts is the school librarian.)

"Oh, that's fine. Well, goodnight, Mary Anne."

"Goodnight, Dad."

He closed my door. I could hear his footsteps as he went back downstairs.

I know my dad loves me, and I know the reason he's strict is that he wants to show everybody I can be a well-brought-up young lady even without a mother, but sometimes I just wish things were different.

I took my torch out of my desk drawer, turned off my light and tiptoed to my window, waiting for Kristy to do the same. I planned to signal I'M SORRY to her. I stood at my window for fifteen minutes, but her shade remained drawn.

I knew then that she was *very* angry.

Chapter 3

The next morning I woke up feeling sad. Kristy had never stayed mad at me for so long. Then again, I had never called her the biggest, bossiest know-it-all in the world. As I got dressed for school, though, I tried to convince myself that the members of the Babysitters Club couldn't stay mad for long. After all, we had a business to run. Surely things would get straightened out in time for our meeting the next day.

When breakfast was over, I kissed my father goodbye and headed out of the front door. I hoped he wouldn't see that I was walking to school alone. If he did, he would know that something was wrong.

I had walked to school alone only six times since kindergarten. Four of those times were days Kristy was home sick; once was when she and her family left for Florida the day before spring vacation started; and once was the day after the

Thomases announced that they were getting divorced, and Kristy had been too upset to go to school.

Sometimes Claudia walked with us; sometimes she didn't. However, since just after we started the Babysitters Club, Kristy, Claudia, Stacey and I had been walking to and from school together almost every day.

I reached the pavement and paused in front of Kristy's house, trying to decide whether to ring her bell and ask to talk to her. In the end, I just kept on walking. Basically, I'm a coward. I didn't want to have a scene with her in front of her family.

I walked quickly to school, keeping my eyes peeled for Kristy, Claudia or Stacey. But I didn't see them. A horrible thought occurred to me: maybe they'd all made up, and I was the only one they were still mad at. With a sinking feeling in my stomach, I entered school.

The very first person I saw was Kristy! She was not with Claudia and Stacey, so I began to feel a bit better.

I waved to her.

Kristy looked right at me. I'm sure she did. She saw me wave.

But she tossed her head in the air, turned around and flounced down the hall. I followed her, since my classroom is next to hers, but I tried to keep a safe distance between us.

As I neared my classroom, I spotted Claudia coming down the hall towards Kristy and me.

"Hey, Kristy!" Claudia called.

Oh, no, I thought. They *have* made up.

But Kristy ignored Claudia.

"*Kristy*," Claudia said again.

"Are you talking to me?" Kristy asked icily. "Or to some other job-hog?"

Claudia's face clouded over. "No, you're the only job-hog I see at the moment."

"Then get a mirror," snapped Kristy.

Claudia looked as if she was preparing some sort of nasty retort, but before she could think of a really good one, Kristy walked into her classroom and slammed the door shut behind her.

I wondered whether it was safe to approach Claudia. After all, she had wanted to make up with Kristy. But just then, the bell rang.

Claudia disappeared into her classroom; I disappeared into mine.

The morning passed slowly. I couldn't concentrate. In my head, I wrote notes of apology to my friends. I realized that I must still be mad at them, though, because some of the notes weren't very nice:

26

Dear Stacey,
I'm really, really sorry you called me a shy little baby. I hope you're sorry, too. . .

Dear Kristy,
I'm sorry you're the biggest, bossiest know-it-all in the world, but what can I do about it? Have you considered seeking professional help?

Dear Claudia,
I'm sorry I called you a stuck-up job-hog. You don't deserve that, and I didn't really mean it. I hope you can forgive me.
Love,
Mary Anne

Now *that* was a note I could send.

In English class, I finished my work early. I carefully removed a fresh piece of loose-leaf paper from the middle of my notebook, and took my special cartridge pen from my bag. The cartridge was filled with peacock-blue ink, and the nib on the pen made my handwriting look like scrolly, swirly calligraphy.

Slowly, making sure each word looked perfect and was spelled correctly, I printed the note to Claudia. Then I waved it back and forth to dry the ink, folded it twice (making the creases straight and even) and tucked it in my bag. I would give it to her at lunchtime.

My knees felt weak as I made my way to the canteen a few minutes later. I'd know right away whether Stacey and Claudia had made up, or if they were still mad, too. They always sat with the same kids – a sophisticated group that included *boys*.

The first thing I did when I entered the canteen was look around to see what was what with my friends. I found Claudia and Stacey's table. There was the usual bunch, or almost the usual bunch: Pete, Howie, Rick, Dori, Emily and Stacey. But no Claudia.

So. Claudia and Stacey hadn't made up, either.

I scanned the room and finally found Claudia. She was sitting with Trevor Sandbourne. Just the two of them. Trevor is this boy she likes and goes out with sometimes. Claudia was leaning on her elbows, her hair falling over her shoulders, whispering to Trevor. He was listening with a smile on his face. They looked very private and very cosy.

I edged around a crowded table towards the one where Kristy and I always sit with the Shillaber twins, Mariah and Miranda. It was a round table with four chairs, perfect for our little group. But halfway there, I stopped. Kristy and the twins were already at the table. They had spread their lunches everywhere so that there wasn't an inch of available space. Furthermore, they'd removed the fourth chair, or lent it to a crowded table, or something. It didn't matter what. The point was that they hadn't saved a place for me.

I watched my friends for a moment. Kristy was facing me. She was talking away a mile a minute and Mariah and Miranda were giggling.

Kristy glanced up and saw me. She began talking even more earnestly. Then she gestured for the twins to lean towards her, and she made a great show of whispering in their ears and laughing loudly.

I turned around.

Suddenly, I felt like a new kid at school. I didn't know who else to sit with. Ever since middle school began, I'd been eating with Kristy, Mariah and Miranda.

I knew that if Kristy were in my shoes, she'd just join some other group of kids, even if she didn't know them very well. But I'd die of embarrassment first. I could never do that.

I walked around the canteen until I found an empty table. I plopped down in a chair and opened my lunch bag. Since I pack my own lunch, I never have to eat things I don't like, such as liver-wurst sandwiches. On the other hand, there are never any surprises. Treats, yes; surprises, no.

I spread a paper napkin on the table and arranged my lunch on it: peanut butter sandwich, apple juice in a box, crisps, banana. I looked it over and realized I wasn't hungry.

I was still staring at it when a voice next to me said, "Excuse me, could I sit here?"

I glanced up. Standing uncertainly by my side was a tall girl with the blondest hair I had ever seen. It was so pale it was almost white, and it hung, straight and silky, to her rear end.

"Sure," I said, waving my hand at all the empty chairs.

She sat down with a sigh, placing a tray in front of her. I looked at her lunch and decided I was glad I had brought mine. I knew Stacey and Claudia think Kristy and I are babies because we still bring our lunches to school, but the macaroni casserole on the girl's tray looked really disgusting. And it was surrounded by mushy, bright orange carrots, a limp salad, and a roll that you'd need a chainsaw to slice.

The girl smiled shyly at me. "You must be new, too," she said.

"New?" I blushed. Why else would I be sitting alone? "Oh," I stammered, "um, no. It's just – my friends are all . . . absent today."

"Oh." The girl sounded disappointed.

"Are – are you new?" I asked after a moment.

She nodded. "This is my second day here. Nobody ever wants the new kid to sit at their table. And I feel embarrassed sitting alone. I thought I'd found the perfect solution – another new kid."

I smiled. "Well, I don't mind if you sit with me. Even if I'm not new."

The girl smiled back. She wasn't exactly pretty, I decided, but she was pleasant, which was more important. Especially considering three *un*pleasant people I could think of.

"My name's Dawn," she said. "Dawn Schafer."

"Dawn," I repeated. "That's such a pretty name. I'm Mary Anne Spier."

"Hi, Mary Anne Spier." Dawn's blue eyes, which were almost as pale as her hair, sparkled happily.

"Did you just move here?" I asked. "Or did you switch schools or something?"

"Just moved here," she replied. "Last week." She began to eat slowly and methodically, taking first a bite of macaroni stuff, then a bite of carrots, then a bite of salad. She worked her way around the plate in a circle. "Our house is still a mess," she went on. "Packing cartons everywhere. Yesterday it took me twenty minutes to find my brother for dinner."

I giggled. At that moment, I happened to look up and see Kristy across the canteen. She was watching me. As soon as I caught her eye, she began talking to Mariah and Miranda again, making it look as if they were having the time of their lives without me.

Well, two can play that game, I thought. Even though I have never been much good at talking to people I don't know well, I leaned across the table and put my head next to Dawn's conspiratorially.

"You want to know who the weirdest kid in school is?"

She nodded eagerly.

He happened to be sitting at the table next to Kristy's. I took advantage of that to point in her direction. "It's Alexander Kurtzman. The one wearing the three-piece suit. See him?" I whispered.

Dawn nodded.

"Don't ever try to butt in front of him on the

lunch queue. Don't even try to get in *back* of him, unless he's at the end of the queue. His hobby is obeying rules."

It was Dawn's turn to laugh. "Who else should I know about?" she asked.

I pointed out a few other kids. We spent the rest of the lunch hour whispering and laughing. Twice I caught Kristy's eye. She looked absolutely poisonous. I knew I wasn't helping our fight, but I kind of liked the idea of getting even with her for not letting me sit at our table.

"Hey, do you want to come over to my house after school tomorrow?" Dawn asked.

"Well . . . well, sure," I replied. It felt so strange to be talking with somebody besides Kristy, Claudia, Stacey or the Shillabers. I wasn't sure that I had ever made a new friend all on my own. Mariah and Miranda had originally been friends Kristy had made, Stacey had been a friend of Claudia's, and I had just grown up with Kristy and Claudia.

"Oh, that's wonderful!" exclaimed Dawn. She must have been really lonely.

I began to feel guilty. I knew full well that one reason I wanted to go over to Dawn's house was to make Kristy (and Stacey and Claudia) mad.

I hoped Kristy would see me leaving school

with Dawn the next afternoon. I hoped she would be surprised. I hoped she would be mad (madder than she already was). I even hoped she'd be a little hurt.

"That would be fun," I added. "Where do you live?"

"Burnt Hill Road."

"That's not too far from me! I live on Bradford Court."

"Great! We can watch a movie."

"OK!"

Dawn and I got up and cleared our places.

"Want to eat lunch again tomorrow?" asked Dawn. "Or will your friends be back?"

I paused. What if we'd all made up by the next day? I decided to cross that bridge when I came to it. "I don't know," I answered.

"It doesn't really matter anyway," said Dawn quietly.

"OK. Well . . . see you."

"See you."

We left the canteen.

I didn't see Kristy, Claudia or Stacey again until school let out that day. Just after the last bell rang, I was standing in the front doorway of Stoneybrook Middle School, looking out across the lawn.

Then I saw them, all three of them. They were walking home from school, each one alone, each one still probably mad.

I set out slowly after them. It wasn't until I got home that I realized I had never given Claudia the note I'd written.

Chapter 4

The first thing I thought when I woke up the next morning was, it's Wednesday. Today is a club-meeting day. We can't stay mad much longer or we won't be able to hold the meeting. And we've never missed a meeting. Suddenly, I was sure our fight was over.

I was so sure that, on my way to school, I stopped at Kristy's house and rang her doorbell. I thought we could walk to school together and apologize to each other.

Ding-dong.

David Michael answered the door. "Hi, Mary Anne!" he said.

"Hi," I replied. "Is Kristy still here?"

"Yup," said David Michael, "she's just—"

"I am *not* here!" I heard Kristy call from the living room.

"Yes, you are. You're right—"

"David Michael, come here for a sec," said Kristy.

David Michael left the front hall.

A few seconds later, I heard footsteps tip-toeing towards the hall. The front door slammed shut in my face.

I stood on the Thomases' stoop, shaking.

Then I turned and crossed the lawn.

All the way to school I kept hearing Kristy's angry voice and the door slamming. Well, I thought, there's still Dawn. Dawn wasn't the same as Kristy or my other friends, but she was something.

We ate lunch together after all. "Your friends are absent again?" Dawn asked. She looked sceptical.

"Yeah," I replied. I decided not even to go into it.

I looked around the canteen for the other members of the Babysitters Club. Things were a bit different that day. Kristy was still eating with the Shillabers, but the empty chair had been filled by another friend of theirs, Jo Deford. Claudia and Trevor were sitting with Rick and Emily. At the opposite end of their long table were Dori, Howie, Pete and Stacey. Every so often, Stacey would look up and give Claudia the evil eye, or Claudia would whisper something to Trevor and then look in Stacey's direction and laugh. Once, she stuck her tongue out at Stacey.

Things were worse than ever. I wasn't surprised that Kristy was holding a grudge, but I had sort of expected Stacey and Claudia to make up, or at least to pretend to have made up. I never thought I'd see the day when cool Claudia would stick her tongue out at somebody in front of Trevor Sandbourne.

"Boy," I said under my breath.

"What?" asked Dawn.

I sighed. "Nothing."

When the bell rang at the end of the day, I made a dash for the front door of school. I was supposed to meet Dawn there and was trying to figure out just how to time things so that Kristy would be sure to see me walking off with my new friend. I decided that I should simply meet Dawn and dawdle. As it happened, things worked out better than I could have hoped.

Almost as soon as I reached the door, kids started streaming past me. I kept my eyes glued to the crowded hallway. After a few moments, I spotted Kristy. She spotted me at the same time and made a face that was a cross between a scowl and a sneer. So what did I do? I smiled. Not at Kristy, but at Dawn, who happened to be right in front of her. I'm sure Kristy thought I was trying to make up with her again.

Boy, was she surprised when Dawn called, "Hi, Mary Anne!" and ran up to me.

"Hi," I replied. I flashed another smile. And as we headed out the door I looked over my shoulder in time to see Kristy standing open-mouthed behind me.

Dawn and I walked across the lawn, talking away a mile a minute. We passed Claudia and Trevor on the way, which only made the afternoon more worthwhile, as far as I could see.

Dawn's new house turned out to be very old. "It's a farmhouse," she told me, "and it was built in seventeen ninety-five."

"Wow!" I said. "You're kidding! Gosh, you were lucky to be able to buy such an old house."

"Yeah, I think so. Even though it needs a lot of work, and it's not very big. You'll see."

We walked through the front door. "If my dad were here," said Dawn, "he'd have to duck."

I looked up and saw that the top of the door frame wasn't far above my head. "People were shorter in seventeen ninety-five," explained Dawn.

I stepped inside, pulling the door closed behind me. I was standing in the middle of a room strewn with packing cartons – some empty, some half-empty, some still unopened – mountains of wadded-up newspaper, and a jumble of, well, *things*. I think we were in the living room, but I could see dishes, toys, sheets and blankets, a shower curtain, a bicycle tyre and a can of peaches.

"My mother isn't very organized yet," said Dawn. "Actually ever. Mom!" she called. "Mom, I'm home!"

"I'm in the kitchen, honey."

Dawn and I stepped over and around things, and managed to reach the kitchen unharmed.

I could see what Dawn meant about the house being small. The kitchen wasn't even big enough for a table and chairs. And it was dark, the window being blocked off by some overgrown yew bushes outside.

A pretty woman with short, curly hair that was every bit as light as Dawn's was standing at the counter slowly turning the pages of a large photo album.

Dawn took a look at the mess (the kitchen was as jumbly as the living room had been) and then at the photo album. "Mom!" she cried. "What are you doing?"

Mrs Schafer looked up guiltily. "Oh, honey," she said. "I keep getting sidetracked. I was working away, and I unpacked this album and an envelope full of pictures marked FOR PHOTO ALBUM, and I just had to stop and put them in."

Dawn smiled and shook her head. "I don't know, Mom. The way we're going, we might as well leave the house like it is. Then, if we ever move again, we could just throw the things back in the boxes."

Mrs Schafer laughed.

"Mom, this is my friend Mary Anne. We eat lunch together."

Mrs Schafer shook my hand. "Hi, Mary Anne. Nice to meet you. I do apologize for the mess. If you go up to Dawn's room, though, you'll find the one civilized spot in the house. Dawn had her bedroom cleaned, unpacked and organized the day after we moved in."

Dawn shrugged. "What can I say? I'm neat."

"Would you like a snack, girls?" asked Mrs Schafer.

"Is there actual food?" asked Dawn.

"Well," her mother replied, "there is actual grape jelly and an actual can of peaches."

"We've been eating out," Dawn told me, "in case you couldn't tell." She turned to her mother. "I think we'll skip the snack, Mom. But thanks."

Dawn and I went upstairs. Everything was

little or low: a small dining room; a narrow, dark stairway leading to a narrow, dark hall. At the end of the hall was Dawn's bedroom, also small, with a low ceiling and a creaky floor.

"Wow, I like your room," I said, "but, gosh, the colonists must have been midgets."

"Maybe," said Dawn. "But there are two good things about this room. One is this." She showed me a small, round window near the ceiling. "I don't know why it's there, but I love it."

"Kind of like a porthole," I said.

Dawn nodded. "The other thing is this." She flicked some switches and the room was flooded with brilliant light. "I can't stand dim rooms," she explained, "so Mom let me get lots of lamps and I put one-hundred-watt bulbs in all of them. I just hope the wiring in this old place can take it."

"Hey!" I exclaimed. "You have a big TV in your room! Boy, are you lucky."

"Well, it's only temporary, until the rest of the house is in order. Then it goes downstairs to the living room. What movie do you want to see?"

"What do you have?"

"Practically everything. My mom's a movie nut."

"Well," I said, "you probably don't have *The Parent Trap*, do you?"

"Of course we do. That was the last thing

she bought before—"

"Before what?" I asked.

Dawn lowered her eyes. "Before the divorce," she whispered. "That's why we moved here. Because Mom and Dad got divorced."

"Why did you move *here*?"

"Mom's parents live here. My mother grew up in Stoneybrook."

"Oh! So did my dad. I wonder if they knew each other."

"What's your dad's name?"

"Richard Spier. What's your mom's name? I mean, what was her name before she got married?"

"Sharon, um, Porter."

"I'll have to ask my father. Wouldn't it be funny if they knew each other?"

"Yeah." Dawn was still staring at the floor.

"Hey," I said, "I guess it's awful when your parents split up, but there's nothing *wrong* with it, you know. Lots of kids have divorced parents. Kristy Thomas, my be – my next-door neighbour, has been a 'divorced kid' for years. And her mom dates this nice divorced man. And—" (I was about to tell her that the parents of the Shillaber twins were divorced, but I didn't really want to talk about the twins.) "And, I mean, I don't care that your parents are divorced."

Dawn smiled slightly. "Where did your mother grow up?" she asked. I guess she wanted to change the subject.

"In Maryland, but she's dead. She died a long time ago."

"Oh." Dawn flushed. Then she started the movie. Soon we were wrapped up in *The Parent Trap*.

"What a great movie," said Dawn with a sigh when it was over.

"I know. One of my favourites." I looked at my watch. It was five-fifteen. "I better go," I said. "This was really fun."

"Yeah, it was. I'm glad you came over," said Dawn.

"Me, too."

We clattered down the midget staircase.

"See you tomorrow!" I called as I left. I ran all the way to Claudia's house. My stomach was tied up in knots. It was time for a meeting of the Babysitters Club.

I had no idea what to expect.

Chapter 5

On the way to the Kishis' house, I told myself that if Claudia answered the door, it would be a good sign. It would be easy for her to let someone else answer it, so if she made the effort, then it probably meant she wasn't so mad any more.

I rang the bell. Mimi opened the door. She looked worried. "Hello, Mary Anne," she said solemnly.

"Hi, Mimi." I hesitated. Usually, I run right upstairs. "Claudia's here, isn't she?"

"Yes, of course. Stacey is here, too. . ."

I knew she wanted to say something more but was too tactful.

"Well, I'll go on up, too. See you later, Mimi." I walked up the stairs, dashed by Janine's room, and entered Claudia's.

There were Stacey and Claudia. Stacey was sitting cross-legged on the bed, staring at her hands. Claudia was seated stiffly in her director's chair, gazing out of the window. Neither one spoke when I entered the room.

Remembering what had happened at Kristy's house that morning, I decided not to be the one to make the first move. I sat down tentatively on the floor.

The phone rang. Claudia was nearest to it, so she took the call. "Hello, the Babysitters Club. . . Oh, hi. . . Saturday morning? . . . OK . . . OK. I'll call you right back. . . Goodbye."

Finally, I thought. Now someone will have to say something.

Claudia hung up the phone. "The Johanssens. They need someone for Charlotte on Saturday morning. Who's free?"

"I am," said Stacey to her hands.

"Mary Anne?"

I shook my head.

"I'm not, either," said Claudia. "I guess it's yours, Stacey."

"Fine." Stacey managed to look pleased through her anger. Charlotte is her favourite kid.

"What about Kristy?" I asked.

"She's not here," said Claudia shortly. "And she knows the rules. She *made* the rules. If she doesn't phone to tell us she'll be late or she can't make it, then she misses out on jobs. I'll call Dr

Johanssen and tell her that *she*" (Claudia shot a dirty look at Stacey) "will be babysitting." When she turned to dial the phone, Stacey stuck her tongue out at her.

Claudia finished the call and hung up. No one said a word.

A few minutes later, the phone rang again. When it was on its third ring, Claudia said, "Somebody else get it this time. I'm not a slave."

I answered it. "Hello? . . . Oh, hi, Mrs Thomas. Is Kristy sick or something? . . . She's where? . . . Oh. No, it's not important. . . For David Michael? Sure, I'll call you right back." I hung up. "Kristy," I said, in case anybody was interested, "is over at the Shillabers' house, and Mrs Thomas needs someone to watch David Michael on Thursday afternoon. . . I'm free."

"So am I," said Claudia.

"So am I," said Stacey.

Uh-oh. When that happens, we usually start saying things like, "Well, I have two other jobs this week, so you can take this one," or "I know you haven't had a chance to sit for David Michael in a while, so you take it."

Somehow, I didn't think anybody was going to say anything like that.

I was right.

Instead, Claudia cut out three scraps of paper, drew a star on one, folded them in half, tossed them in a shoebox and said, "Everybody pick one. The person who gets the star sits for David Michael."

Claudia chose the star.

"Hey!" cried Stacey. "You knew which one it was!"

"I did not!" exclaimed Claudia. "How would I know that?"

"You made the scraps of paper."

"Are you calling me a cheater?"

"You said it, I didn't."

Oh, brother, I thought. Here we go again.

In the end, Stacey allowed Claudia to keep the job. The phone rang two more times before the end of our meeting, and we managed to set up the babysitting jobs without actual violence.

At precisely six o'clock, Stacey stood up and marched out of Claudia's room without so much as a word. Claudia and I looked at each other, but Claudia didn't say anything, either, so I followed Stacey. Mimi watched us walk silently out of the front door.

As we stepped on to the lawn, Stacey broke into a run, but for some reason, I turned around and looked back at the house. Claudia was in her window. I hesitated. Then I waved to her.

She flashed me a hopeful smile and waved back.

On impulse, I ran up the Kishis' steps again, opened the door, called Mimi, and handed her the note I had written to Claudia. Then I ran across the street to my house.

My father hadn't come home yet. When the numbers on the digital clock flipped to six-fifteen and he still wasn't home, I took it as a sign and decided to call Claudia. If I didn't talk to her before supper, I'd have to wait until the next morning.

I dialled her private number.

"Hello?"

"Hi, Claudia," I said nervously. "It's Mary Anne."

"Oh. Hi."

"Well, I—"

"I got your note. Mimi gave it to me. Thanks."

"You're welcome."

"I forgive you. And I'm sorry I got mad, too," Claudia said rather stiffly.

"Well. . ." I didn't know what to say next. Was our fight over? "Well . . . one reason I'm calling is Kristy. Since she went to the Shillabers' today," I said, "and skipped our meeting, I guess that means she doesn't want to be part of the club. I mean, I don't know. . ."

"I guess for a while, anyway, she doesn't want to be part of it," agreed Claudia. "What should we do about the club then? I mean, she *is* president."

"I know. I was thinking about that. We shouldn't *really* keep taking jobs without asking her whether she wants them."

"Yeah. On the other hand, she should come to the meetings."

Claudia didn't say anything.

"Claud?"

"I just don't know what to do. Stacey is almost as mad as Kristy is."

"What's strange," I said, "is that Kristy hasn't said she wants the club to go out of business. She's just ignoring it – and the club is *her* business. Why would she let us run it without her when we're the ones she's mad at?"

Claudia was probably shrugging her shoulders. "Maybe you and I should talk to Stacey and Kristy tomorrow and see what they want to do. We certainly can't keep having meetings like the one we just had. If you talk to Kristy, I'll talk to Stacey."

"All right," I agreed, "but it's not going to be easy." I didn't tell Claudia about Kristy and the door-slamming. I figured she was having just as much trouble with Stacey as I was having with Kristy.

How was I supposed to talk to Kristy? I didn't want to go to her house again, and I had a feeling that if I called her on the phone, she'd simply hang up on me. The only thing left to do was to surprise her.

I ambushed her at school the next morning as she came out of the girls' room. I stepped right in front of her.

"Ex*cuse* me," said Kristy haughtily.

My heart was pounding like a jackhammer, but I stood my ground. "I have to talk to you," I said.

"No, you don't."

"Yes, I do."

"No."

"Yes."

"No."

"We have to decide what to do about the club. Are you out of it?"

"*Out* of it? It's my club."

"Exactly."

"What do you mean 'exactly'?"

"I mean, it's your club, but you didn't go to the meeting yesterday."

"It's my club so I didn't *have* to go to the meeting."

"But you missed out on a lot of good jobs."

Kristy kicked at a piece of wadded-up paper that was littering the hall.

"I mean," I went on, "we weren't going to call the Shillabers' house every time a job came in, to see if you wanted it."

"You should have," she said sullenly.

It was getting harder for me to argue with her. I was used to giving in on things. I drew in a deep breath. "Not according to the rules."

"Yeah."

"Anyway, Claudia decided that we better figure out how to run the club while" (I had started to say "while we're all mad at each other" and realized that that wasn't very tactful) "while. . ."

"While we're all mad at each other?" suggested Kristy.

"Well . . . yes. I think Claudia and I are the only ones speaking to each other, so yest—"

"You and Claudia are speaking?"

"Yes."

"Brother. Whatever happened to faithful friends?"

"What *happened* to them?" I cried. "They had doors slammed in their faces, that's what!"

"OK, OK, OK. Well, how about if we take turns answering the phone in Claudia's room at meeting times? You go one day, I'll go the next. . ."

"What about offering the jobs around? If we have to call each member of the club to tell her about each job call that comes in, we'll end up talking to each other more than ever that way."

Kristy looked to the ceiling for help. "When a club member is on duty, she takes on as many jobs as she can. Then the only jobs she has to offer around are the ones she can't take herself. How does that sound?"

"Fair," I said. "I'll tell Claudia."

Kristy nodded.

"Hi, Mary Anne!" called a voice from down the hall.

It was Dawn.

I turned around and waved. She ran towards me. "How are you? Yesterday was fun, wasn't it?"

"Great," I agreed. "And I was wondering. Do you want to come over on Saturday? Maybe we could make fudge or bake cookies." I glanced at Kristy. If she opened her eyes any wider, her eyeballs would roll out and land on the floor.

"Sure!" exclaimed Dawn.

"Good! See you at lunch?"

"See you at lunch." Dawn trotted happily down the hall.

Kristy was still staring at me. At last she managed to say, "You just invited her over to your house."

"Right."

"But you never ask anyone over except *me*. You don't usually even invite Claudia or Stacey over."

I shrugged. "Dawn's a good friend."

Kristy narrowed her eyes. I think she knew what game I was playing, because she chose that moment to say, "Oh, by the way, Mom extended my babysitting hours. Now I can stay out as late as Stacey: ten o'clock on weekends, nine-thirty on weeknights."

It was my turn to widen my eyes. *Ten o'clock?* Kristy could stay out until *ten*? That meant I had to be home earlier than any other club member.

I could feel my face flush. Kristy might just as well have pinned a sign to me that said BABY because that's what I was. The only baby in the Babysitters Club.

Kristy walked off, smirking.

I hung my head, mad at Kristy and mad at my father.

I knew I had to do something – but what?

Chapter 6

According to our new emergency operating procedures, the Babysitters Club meetings were being handled by one club member at a time. Friday was my first day. Since Claudia and I were speaking, she stayed in her room with me, but we stuck to Kristy's new rules, and I took all but one of the jobs that afternoon.

The last call that came in was from a woman named Mrs Prezzioso. I knew the Prezziosos slightly. They live on Burnt Hill Road not far from Dawn, and are friends with the Pikes, the eight-kid family our club members often sit for. I had met the Prezziosos several times at the Pikes'.

"Hello, the Babysitters Club," I said when I answered Mrs Prezzioso's call.

"Hello. This is Madeleine Prezzioso over on Burnt Hill Road. To whom am I speaking?"

To whom was she speaking? "This is Mary Anne Spier," I said.

"Oh, Mary Anne. Hello, dear. How are you?"

"Fine, thank you," I replied politely. "How are you?" I should mention here that the Prezziosos, all three of them, look extremely prim and proper – but Mrs Prezzioso is the only one who acts that way, too. She's fussy and fastidious, kind of like the neat half of *The Odd Couple*. She's always polite, and she usually appears to have stepped right out of the pages of one of those magazines that gives tips on getting out hard-to-remove stains and baking the perfect loaf of zucchini bread. She buys three-piece suits and monogrammed handkerchiefs for Mr Prezzioso. And Jenny, their three-year-old daughter. . . Well, Mrs Prezzioso dresses her as if every day were Easter Sunday. She puts ribbons in her hair and lacy socks on her feet. Mrs P. probably thinks *jeans* is a dirty word.

Poor Jenny doesn't seem to be the prim, fastidious type at all. Neither does Mr P. When I'm around him, I usually have the feeling that he'd rather be dozing in front of the TV in dungarees, a T-shirt, and mismatched socks. And Jenny tries hard, but she just isn't what her mother wants her to be.

Mrs P. and I chatted for a minute or so and then got down to business. "I know this is last-minute, dear," she said, "but I need a sitter for Sunday afternoon. Mr Prezzioso and I have been invited to a tea."

"What time does it start?" I asked.

"Four o'clock. I should think we'd be home by six or six-thirty."

"OK, I'll be there."

"That's wonderful, dear. Thank you. I'll see you at four. Goodbye!"

I hung up the phone thoughtfully. The afternoon at the Prezziosos' could be pretty interesting.

On Sunday afternoon I rang the Prezziosos' doorbell promptly at three-thirty. Jenny came flying to answer it. I could hear her calling hello and fiddling with the locks. After a few moments, she pulled it open – but the chain was still attached. *CRACK!*

"Jenny!" a voice exclaimed behind her. "Did you ask who was there before you opened the door?"

"No, Mommy."

"Well, what are you supposed to do when the doorbell rings?"

"Say, 'Who is it?'"

"Then please do that." The door closed. The locks slid back into place.

"Mary Anne," Mrs Prezzioso called, "would you mind ringing the bell again, please?"

I sighed. *Ding-dong.*

"Who is it?" asked Jenny's voice.

"It's me, Mary Anne Spier."

"Are you a stranger?"

"No, I'm your babysitter."

"Now can I let her in, Mommy?"

"Yes, sweetheart. That was very good."

At last the door opened. I stepped inside and took off my coat. Both Mrs P. and Jenny were all dressed up. Mrs P. looked exactly as if she were off to a fancy tea. But Jenny seemed a bit overdressed for an afternoon of stories and games and fun. She was wearing a frilly white dress trimmed with yards of lavender lace and ribbon, matching lavender socks, and shiny black patent-leather Mary Janes. Her hair had been curled, and was pulled back from either side of her face by barrettes from which long streamers flowed. Really, her mother ought to just pose her in a display case somewhere.

"Hello, Mary Anne," Mrs P. greeted me.

"Hi," I replied. "Hi, Jenny."

Jenny looked wistfully at the blue jean skirt I was wearing. "I like your skirt, Mary Anne," she said.

"Now, Jenny," Mrs P. said briskly, "it's a very pretty skirt, I'm sure, but not as pretty as my little angel in her brand-new dress!" She pulled Jenny to her and covered her with loud kisses. "Who's my little angel?" she asked.

Jenny's face was smushed up against her mother's arm. "Mmmphh," she said.

Mrs P. tried again. "Who's my little angel?"

Jenny drew away from her. "I am, Mommy."

"And what are you made of?"

"Sugar 'n' spice 'n' all that's nice."

Gag, gag. I remembered another nursery rhyme. That one went, "There was a little girl who had a little curl, right in the middle of her forehead; when she was good, she was very, very good, and when she was bad she was horrid."

"Isn't our angel pretty today?" Mrs Prezzioso asked me.

Our angel? "Yes, she sure is," I replied.

Jenny smiled sweetly.

"All right, I'm ready, Madeleine," boomed a voice from the stairs. Mr P. came thundering down from the first floor.

"OK, angel, you be a good girl for your sitter. Will you promise me that?" He tossed Jenny in the air and she squealed with delight.

"Oh, be careful!" cried Mrs Prezzioso. "Her new dress . . . and your new ascot. Nick, please."

(What's an ascot?)

Mr P. returned Jenny safely to the ground. "Well, let's go. Thanks for coming over, Mary Lou."

"Mary *Anne*," Jenny corrected him.

Mrs P. stood in front of her husband. She straightened his tie, adjusted his jacket and arranged the handkerchief in his pocket so that it was absolutely straight and the monogram was perfectly centred.

Then she turned around and stood next to her husband. "How do we look?" she asked me.

I glanced at Jenny. Jenny was watching me.

I blushed. "You look. . ." Somehow "very nice" didn't sound like enough. "You look like a picture out of a magazine," I finally said. And they did, all posed and stiff.

Mrs P. appeared confused, but recovered quickly. "Why, thank you, dear."

There was a pause. "You're welcome," I said, to fill the silence.

"Now, we'll be at the Elliot Taggarts' this afternoon," said Mrs Prezzioso. "Their number is written on the message board in the kitchen, and the emergency numbers are right next to the phone. If we're not home by six o'clock, you can give Jenny a sandwich for supper."

"OK," I said. Jenny and I walked her parents to the back door. "Have fun!" I called as they climbed into their car.

I closed the door and leaned against it for a few seconds. "Well," I said to Jenny, "what do you want to do first?"

Jenny flopped on the sofa in the playroom and pouted. "Nothing."

"Oh, come on," I said brightly, "there must be something you want to do. We have two hours to play."

Jenny stuck out her lower lip and shook her head. "Unh-unh."

"Well, in that case," I said, "I'll just play with the Kid-Kit by myself."

Kid-Kits were something Kristy had dreamed up to make us babysitters as much fun as possible for our charges. Each of us had decorated a cardboard carton, which we'd labelled KID-KIT. We kept the boxes filled with books and games (our own) plus activity books that we paid for out of our club dues. The kids we babysit for love the Kid-Kits and look forward to our visits because of them.

But Jenny had never seen one. "What's a Kid-Kit?" she asked.

"Oh, just something I brought with me." I'd left it on the front porch so I could surprise Jenny with it after the Prezziosos left. I retrieved it and sat down on the floor in the middle of the playroom. I opened the box and began pulling things out: three books, two games, a box of Colourforms, a sticker book, and a paint-with-water book. I turned my back on Jenny and began peeling balloons off the back page of the sticker book.

After a moment, Jenny left the sofa and edged towards me and the Kid-Kit. She watched me put stickers in the book. Then she glanced at the things I'd pulled out. She opened the box of Colourforms. It was an old set of mine called Mrs Cookie's Kitchen. She touched the flat plastic pots and pans and food. Then she put the lid back on the box.

"I can play with this stuff?" she asked.

"Sure. That's why I brought it."

"I can play with anything I want?"

"Of course."

"Is this a painting book?"

I glanced up. "Oh . . . yes. Here, how about the stickers? Don't they look like fun?"

"I WANT TO PAINT!"

"OK, OK." I looked at Jenny's pristine white dress. I looked at the paint-with-water book.

62

Wasn't the point of painting with water that it wasn't messy?

I went to the kitchen and half filled a paper cup with water. Then I brought it to Jenny, opened the paint book for her and settled her on the floor. "OK, go to it," I said. "All you have to do is brush water over the pictures, and the colour will appear. Make sure you rinse the brush off pretty often so the colours don't mix together. OK?"

Jenny nodded.

"And . . . be careful," I added.

Jenny was sitting cross-legged, the book spread open in front of her. She dipped the paintbrush in the water and moved it slowly towards the book. Drip, drip, drip. Three wet spots appeared on her dress.

I closed my eyes. It was only water. Still. . .

"Jenny, wouldn't you like to put on play clothes while you paint?" I thought she must own *some*thing more casual than what she had on.

"No."

"No? Not even a smock? We could put it on over your dress."

"No."

"How about one of Mommy's aprons?"

"I DON'T WANT AN APRON!"

I watched Jenny smear the paintbrush over

a big apple on the page. The apple turned red. Jenny lifted the brush and returned it to the cup. So far, so good.

I relaxed a little.

Then Jenny swung the wet brush back to the book. Two faint pink streaks appeared on her dress. Oh, well, I thought. It must come out with water.

But I wasn't sure. I decided that Jenny would have to wear an apron whether she liked it or not, and I dashed into the kitchen. I had just found one when I heard Jenny say, "Oops."

"Jenny?" I called. "What happened?"

There was a pause. "Nothing."

A nothing is usually the worst kind of something. I ran back to Jenny – and gasped. She had spilled the entire cup of water in her lap. A huge pinkish stain was spreading fast.

"Oh, *Jenny*!" I exclaimed.

Jenny stared at me with wide eyes. She looked as if she were daring me to do something.

"OK. Off with your dress. Right now."

"NONONONONONONO!" Jenny threw herself on her stomach and began kicking her legs on the floor.

I took advantage of that to unbutton her dress. "Off it comes," I said. "Then I'll show you some magic."

Jenny stopped kicking and yelling. "Magic?"

"Yeah." I hoped the trick would work.

Jenny let me take her dress off. She followed me into the kitchen and sat on the counter while I held the dress under a stream of water from the tap. She watched as the colour flowed out.

I breathed a sigh of relief. "Does your mommy have a hair dryer?" I asked.

"Yup."

"Come show me where."

So Jenny, giggling, helped me blow-dry her dress. Then I told her that she would *have* to wear play clothes if she wanted to finish painting. She took me to her room, pointed to a drawer in her bureau, and said, "That's where the play clothes are."

I opened the drawer and found myself looking at three piles of neatly folded, spotless, almost-new shirts, blouses and slacks. "These are your play clothes?"

Jenny gave me a look that plainly said, "I told you so."

I closed the drawer. "OK, Jenny-bunny," I said. "Do you want to finish painting?"

"Yes."

"All right. Come on." We went back downstairs and Jenny spent the rest of the afternoon painting in her underwear. I got her dressed just five minutes before the Prezziosos came home.

"How was she?" Mrs P. asked.

I glanced down at Jenny. "An angel," I replied. "An absolute angel."

Jenny smiled at me. Our secret was safe.

Chapter 7

I couldn't stand it any longer. I decided to ask my father if he would extend my babysitting hours. If all the other members of the club were allowed to stay out until ten o'clock, I ought to be able to as well. After all, I was the same age as they were, I was just as responsible as they were, and I had just as much homework as they did.

The one job that I had had to turn down, when I was taking club phone calls the Friday after our fight, had been for a client who needed a sitter until ten o'clock on Saturday night. Kristy had taken the job.

I felt humiliated.

But I was nervous about facing my father. He wouldn't be angry; he just wouldn't see my side, unless I figured out exactly the right way to approach him. And I wasn't sure I'd be able to do that.

But by Monday night, I was ready to talk to

him – no matter what.

Unfortunately, he came home in a bad mood.

"We lost the Cutter case today," he told me. "I can't believe it. I thought it was open-and-shut. The jury was highly unreasonable."

I nodded. "Dad—"

"Honestly, sometimes people can be so unfair. . . No, not unfair, *unthinking*. That's it, unthinking." We were setting the table, getting ready for dinner.

"Dad—" I said again.

"Can you imagine letting someone go who so clearly was guilty of grand larceny?"

I shook my head. "I guess not. . . Dad?"

"What is it, Mary Anne?"

Right then, I should have decided not to pursue the business of later hours, but I'd been planning on it all day. I'd rehearsed what I was going to say. I didn't know if it would work, but I was going to say, very rationally, "Dad, I've been thinking. I'm twelve years old now, and I feel that I could stay out until ten o'clock every now and then when I'm babysitting – not on school nights, of course, because I recognize that I need my sleep, but just on some Friday and Saturday nights."

"Dad, I've been thinking," I said.

The phone rang.

Dad leaped for it. "Hello? . . . Yes, I know. . . I know. . . Right, an appeal. That's what I was think— What? . . . Oh, yes. Definitely. . ." The conversation went on for ten minutes while our frozen pizza finished baking and then began drying out in the oven.

Dad finally got off the phone, and immediately it rang again. When he got off the second time, I practically threw the pizza down in front of him.

"Dad, I want to stay out until ten o'clock when I babysit at night," I blurted out.

My father looked at me blankly. "What? . . . Oh. Mary Anne, no. I'm afraid that's out of the question."

"But, Dad, everyone else gets to."

"I'm sure not *every*one does. You can't possibly be the only sixth-grader who has to be in by nine or nine-thirty."

"Dad, I'm in *seventh* grade, and I *am* the only member of the Babysitters Club who can't stay out till ten. You treat me like a baby, but look at me. I'm halfway through seventh grade. In a year and a half I'll be starting high school."

For a moment, my father looked taken aback. Then a change came over his face. He rubbed his hands over his eyes tiredly. At last he said softly,

"It's not easy for a father to raise a daughter alone. I have to be both a father and a mother. On top of that, I'm not home much. I'm doing the best I can."

"But Kristy and Claudia and Stacey—"

"What Kristy and Claudia and Stacey and their parents do is not our concern."

"That's not fair! Don't you think Mrs Thomas is a good mother? Don't you think Mimi and the Kishis care about Claudia?"

"Those are not the issues," my father said. "The issues are you and me and your bedtime."

"Dad, I am old enough to stay out until ten o'clock. I'm twelve, and I'm very responsible and mature. Don't my teachers always write that on my report card? 'Mary Anne is a joy to have in class. She's responsible and mature.'"

"You don't sound mature at the moment."

I knew I didn't. I was whining. But it was too late to stop. I was on a roll. "I'm also too old to wear my hair in these dumb plaits, and my room looks like a nursery. It's a room for a five-year-old."

My father looked at me sharply. "Young lady, I do not like your tone of voice."

"You know, you're not the only parent who isn't around much," I went on, ignoring him. "Mrs

Thomas is hardly ever home, either, and she has to raise Kristy *and* Kristy's brothers alone, and Sam and Charlie don't have Peter Rabbit all over their bedroom. I'd like to see a few changes around here. I'd like to be allowed to choose my own clothes. I'd like to take my hair out of these plaits. I'd like to wear nail varnish and stockings and lipstick. And if a boy ever asked me to go to the movies or something, I'd like to be able to say yes – without even checking with you first. You know what? Sometimes you don't seem like my father to me. You seem like my jailer."

It was at that exact moment that I knew I'd gone too far.

Sure enough, my father turned his back on me. Then, in the calmest voice imaginable, he said, "Mary Anne, the subject is closed. Please go to your room."

I went. I felt horrible. I knew I'd insulted him, and I hadn't wanted to do that. But what did he think was going to happen if I wore my hair loose or took down Humpty Dumpty? Did he think I'd run away or start hanging around with the wild kids at the mall? And what could happen between nine o'clock and ten o'clock while I was babysitting, that couldn't happen before nine?

I didn't have any answers, but I knew someone

who might – Mimi. She was a patient listener and I often talked to her about things that I might have talked to my mother about. At any rate, I talked to her about things I couldn't discuss with my father.

I paid her a visit after school the next day. I had apologized twice to my father that morning, and he'd said he accepted my apology, but things were a little chilly between us.

"Hi, Mimi," I greeted her, when she answered the bell.

"Hello, Mary Anne," she said solemnly. "How is your scarf coming?"

"Fine. It looks really nice. I hope my father will like it. If I work hard, I could finish it in time for his birthday."

"That would be a nice surprise for him." I shrugged out of my coat, and Mimi hung it in the closet. "Well," she went on, "are you here to see Claudia? She is not at home. I believe she is babysitting for Nina and Eleanor Marshall."

"Oh. No, actually I came to see you. I wondered if we could talk. . ."

"Of course. Please come in. Would you like some tea, Mary Anne?"

"Yes. Thanks." I don't really like tea, but I like

drinking it with Mimi. She fixes it in a special pot and serves it in little cups that don't have any handles. Then she lets me put in all the milk and sugar I want.

I followed her into the kitchen, and Mimi set the tea things on the table and began boiling water. She took some crackers out of a tin and arranged them on a plate.

When everything was ready, we sat down across from each other. Mimi poured the tea, straining the leaves out of my cup, but letting them flow into hers and sink to the bottom. I began adding milk and sugar. Mimi took hers plain – and strong.

"It is very dreary weather," Mimi commented, looking out at the barren trees being lashed about by the wind and soaked by the chilling rain that had fallen all day.

"Yeah," I agreed, feeling sad.

"In this weather," Mimi continued, "I always think of spring. Snowy weather makes me glad for winter, but raw, grey weather makes me wish winter were over. Perhaps we will be lucky and the groundhog will see his shadow."

I smiled. "That would be great."

"And how are you surviving this dreariness?"

I looked at Mimi. Her black hair, which had

long been streaked with white, was pulled away from her face and fastened into a bun just above her neck. She wore no jewellery and no make-up, and her face was wrinkled and creased. I thought she was beautiful. Maybe it was because she always seemed so serene.

"I'm surviving the dreariness OK, I guess," I replied, "but I'm not surviving my father very well. . . Mimi, do you think I act like a normal twelve-year-old?"

"Tell me what you mean by normal."

"You know – like other twelve-year-olds. Am I about as responsible and mature and smart as other twelve-year-olds, and do I have pretty much the same interests they do?"

Now, most adults might have said something like, "That sounds like a loaded question," or "What are you *really* asking?" But Mimi put her teacup down, sat back in her chair and considered me. At last she replied, "Yes, you seem like a normal twelve-year-old to me. You do not wear the clothes that Claudia does, but I do not think that means anything. You are very responsible, and you also seem very mature. But you are serious, too, and I know it is not wise to confuse gravity with maturity."

She had almost lost me, but all that counted

was that she thought I seemed like any other kid my age. "So, Mimi," I went on, "how come I'm not allowed to make my room more grown-up? You know what's on my walls? Alice in Wonderland and Humpty Dumpty. . . Do you know who Humpty Dumpty is?"

"Oh, yes. He is the shattered eggman."

I giggled, then remembered the reason for our discussion and became serious again. "Right, but he's from a Mother Goose nursery rhyme. A *nursery* rhyme, Mimi. Nursery rhymes aren't for twelve-year-olds. They're not even for little kids. They're for *babies*. But Dad won't let me take Humpty down. He won't even let me leave Humpty where he is and put new posters up next to him. He won't let me wear my hair down or put on nail varnish or stay out past nine-thirty at the absolute latest. And Claudia, Stacey and even Kristy are allowed to do all those things – and a lot more. Every time I turn around, I'm facing another one of my father's rules: you can't ride your bike downtown, you can't wear trousers to school, you can't do this or this or this."

I paused to catch my breath.

Mimi raised her eyebrows slightly. "I know it is not easy for you," she said slowly. She sipped her tea. "And I suppose you have heard people say that your father is doing the best he can."

I nodded. It seemed as if everyone in the *world* had said that at some time or other.

"Well, I will tell you something that I have often told my Claudia. If you do not like the way things are, you must change them yourself."

"But I've tried!" I exclaimed.

"Perhaps you have not found the right way yet. If this is truly important to you, then there is a right way to change it. And I know that you, my Mary Anne, will find that way."

At that moment, Claudia burst into the kitchen.

"What did you just say?" she asked accusingly.

"Claudia, you are finished babysitting already?" said Mimi.

Claudia ignored the question. "I heard you!" she cried, glaring at Mimi. "You called *her*," she switched her glare to me, *"my Mary Anne."*

"Why, yes I did," Mimi said quietly.

"But I'm the only one you call yours. You don't even say 'my Janine'. . . I thought I was the only one."

I had rarely seen Claudia so upset. Not when she got bad grades, and not when we thought the Babysitters Agency was going to put our club out of business. But she was standing in front of us with tears running down her cheeks.

Then she turned and ran. I could hear her feet pounding up the stairs and along the hall to her bedroom.

"Oh, no," I said to Mimi.

"Please do not worry," she told me. "That was my fault. I was not thinking. I will talk to Claudia and repair our misunderstanding." Mimi stood up.

I rose, too. "Thank you, Mimi," I said.

Mimi gave me a hug, then headed upstairs. I let myself out of the front door.

What was the right way to change things? I wondered. I knew that I would have to discover it myself.

Chapter 8

Tuesday, January 20

*I am so made! I know this notebook is
for writing up our siting jobs so we can
keep track of club problems. Well, this
is not a sitting job, but I have a club
probleme. Her name is Mary Anne Spier
or as she is otherwise know MY MARY
ANNE. Where does Mary Anne get off
being so chummy with Mimi? It isn't
fair. It's one thing for Mimi to help her
with her nittin k nitting but today they
were sharing tea in the special cups and
Mimi called her MY MARY ANNE.
NO FAIR. So there.*

Wow. Was Claudia ever mad. Mimi had
apologized and tried to explain things to her, but

Claudia stopped talking to me anyway, which meant that once again, not one of the members of the Babysitters Club was talking to the others.

Twice recently, I had tried waiting for Kristy at my window with the torch after my father said goodnight to me. The first time, Kristy's room stayed dark, and the second time, she didn't bother going to the window. Her shade was up, and I could see her in her room – doing her homework, talking to her mother and playing with Louie, the Thomases' collie. But she never once even looked towards her window. How long would our fight go on?

I considered telling Dawn about it, and decided not to.

The next time it was my turn to answer the Babysitters Club phone calls, I didn't have nearly as easy a time as I'd had before. For one thing, Claudia was at home, and she was not pleased to have me in her room. She turned on some music and played it so loudly that the first time the phone rang I almost didn't hear it.

"Hello!" I shouted into the receiver. "Babysitters Club!" I'm sure the person on the other end of the phone said something, but all I could hear was:

"DUM-DE-DUM-DE-DUM DUM. CAN'T LIVE WITHOUT YOU-OU-OU-OU-OU."

"What?" I yelled.

"DE-DOOOO. DE-DOOOO. MY LIFE IS YOU-OU-OU-OU-OU."

"CLAUDIA, CAN YOU PLEASE TURN THAT DOWN?" I shouted.

Claudia ignored me. She began singing along. "DE-DOOOO," she sang, "DE-DOP. IT'S LIFE AT THE TOP, THE TOP!"

I tried putting my finger in one ear. "HELLO?"

Very faintly, I could hear a voice say, "Why are you shouting? Is everything all right?"

"Mrs NEWTON? I MEAN, Mrs Newton, is that you?"

"Yes. Mary Anne? What's all that noise?"

"Oh . . . just some music."

"Well, listen, I need a sitter Wednesday afternoon for Jamie. I'm going to visit a friend for a couple of hours and I'll be taking the baby with me. Is anyone available?"

Claudia's music was between songs, so I could hear a lot better. "I'll have to check," I said. "I know I'm not free."

"Could you check with Kristy first? I think

Jamie would like to see her."

"All right," I agreed – reluctantly.

Darn. I would have to phone Kristy.

"I'll call you right b—"

"OH, MY, MY. OH, MY, MY. MY BABY'S SAD AND SO AM I." The next song blasted on.

Mrs Newton and I hung up.

Just as Claudia's song was picking up pace, Mimi stuck her head in the room. I'm sure she had knocked, but of course we hadn't heard her.

She signalled to Claudia, who turned the volume down – slightly.

"Claudia," she said, "I must ask you to play your music more softly. It is much too loud. Also, I was wondering if you would like to come downstairs and have a cup of tea with me while Mary Anne is answering the phone."

Claudia considered the offer. At last she turned off the music and left with Mimi. On her way out the door, she stuck her tongue out at me.

I stuck mine out at her.

She slammed the door shut.

With shaking fingers, I dialled the Thomases' number.

Kristy answered the phone.

"Hello," I said, "it's Mary Anne Spier."

There was a pause. "Yes?"

I'd thought she'd at least say "hello" back.

"Mrs Newton needs a sitter for Jamie on Wednesday. He wants you. Can you make it?"

"Yup."

"All right, I'll tell her."

"Hey, don't hang up!"

No? Oh, boy. Kristy was going to make the big apology. I couldn't believe it. After all this time, bossy Kristy was going to be the one to give in first, while I, timid Mary Anne, had managed to wait the fight out. Our fight was finally over! I felt so happy at the idea that I practically hugged myself. "Yeah?" I said.

"What time does she want me?"

"Ask her yourself," I said, and hung up. Then I called Mrs Newton back.

The next phone call was from Watson, needing a sitter for Karen and Andrew the following Saturday afternoon. "I know it isn't your club policy," said Watson, "but could you check with Kristy first? I'd sort of like Andrew and Karen to keep seeing her since she *is* going to be their stepsister soon."

"Sure," I replied dully. What else could go wrong? I dialled Kristy's number again. David Michael answered.

"Hello, this is David Michael speaking. Who's calling, please?"

"It's Mary Anne," I told him.

"Hi!" he cried. "When are you going to come over and babysit for me again? Remember the last time you came? We bowled paper cups down the stairs."

"Yeah, that was fun, wasn't it?"

"Yeah!"

"David Michael, can you call Kristy for me, please? I have to talk to her."

"Sure."

When Kristy got on the phone, she didn't say a word. I just guessed that she was there because I heard light breathing.

"Kristy?"

"WHAT?"

"Watson wants you to sit on Saturday – from two-thirty until five," I added pointedly.

"Fine."

"I'll call him back. Goodbye."

We hung up.

The phone rang again. "Hello, the Babysitters Club," I said.

"Hi, Mary Anne. It's Mrs Newton again. I forgot to ask you whether you and Kristy and Claudia and Stacey want to come to Jamie's fourth birthday party. It's in about two weeks, and I'd like you girls to be there as helpers as well as guests. We've invited sixteen children, so I'm going to need lots of help."

"Sure!" I exclaimed. "I mean, if we can make it. It sounds like fun. I'll have to call the other girls."

Mrs Newton gave me the information about the party, and I began to call the club members. Luckily, Stacey wasn't home, so I left a message with Mrs McGill for Stacey to call Mrs Newton.

One down, two to go. I didn't want to call Kristy a third time, but I didn't want to talk to Claudia in person, either.

I flipped a coin. Claudia.

I walked slowly downstairs and found her drinking tea from the special cups with Mimi.

"Claud?" I ventured.

Claudia put her cup down and covered her ears with her hands. "HMM, HMM, HM-HM." She closed her eyes and hummed loudly. "I CAN'T HEAR YOU."

I glanced helplessly at Mimi.

Mimi reached across the table and touched Claudia lightly on the arm. That was all it took for Claudia to act human again. She opened her eyes and uncovered her ears.

"Mrs Newton wants all the members of our

club to be helpers at Jamie's fourth birthday party," I said. I told her when it was. "Do you want to go?"

"Yes," she replied coolly. "I'll go."

"Fine," I answered just as coolly.

But I was beginning to wonder how fine an idea it really was. How could the four of us help out at a party when we wouldn't even talk to each other? Nevertheless, I returned to Claudia's room to call Kristy for the third time.

"What *is* it?" she asked crossly.

I told her about Jamie's party.

Kristy sighed. "Oh, all right. I'll go, too."

"Don't strain yourself," I said. "I can call Mrs Newton and tell her you're busy."

"Don't you dare!"

"I was just trying to help out."

"Oh, sure."

We hung up again.

It was almost six o'clock by then, but I received two more Babysitters Club calls. The first was from Mrs Prezzioso, wanting me to sit for Jenny. I checked our record book, saw that I was free, and told her I'd be glad to sit.

The second call was from Mrs Pike, the mother of the eight kids. The Pikes are good customers, even though they usually just need a sitter for

Claire and Margo and the younger children. The older ones can take care of themselves. However, Mrs Pike's call was not one of her usual ones.

"Hi, Mary Anne," she said. "Listen, Mr Pike and I have been invited to a cocktail party over in Levittown. It'll be an early evening – we'll be back by nine – but we don't want to leave the kids alone while we're out of town, so we need someone to sit for all of them. Actually, we need two someones."

"OK," I said. We'd done that before – sent two sitters over to the Pike brood.

Mrs Pike gave me the information and I said I would call her back in a few minutes when I had found out who else was available. I checked our record book. I couldn't believe it.

The only person free was Kristy.

I didn't bother to sigh or get nervous. I just picked up the phone and dialled.

Kristy answered.

"Hi, it's Mary Anne again," I said in a rush. "The Pikes need two sitters on Friday while they go to a party in Levittown. You and I are the only ones free. We'd be sitting for all the kids. Do you want to do it?"

"With you?"

"Yes."

"Not really."

"Fine. I'll get Dawn Schafer to sit with me. I don't want to let Mrs Pike down."

"You wouldn't dare."

"I'll have to."

"Mary Anne Spier, for someone who's so shy, you sure can be—"

"What? I can be what?"

"Never mind. I'll sit with you."

"We'll have to be mature about it, you know."

"Look who's talking."

"I'm serious, Kristy. We don't want the Pike kids telling their parents that we were fighting or anything."

"I think that would be impossible."

"Why?"

"Because I'm not speaking to you."

"Good," I said. I hung up on her. Then I noted our job in the record book and called Mrs Pike back.

I was not looking forward to babysitting with Kristin Amanda Thomas.

Chapter 9

Saturday, January 31

Yesterday, Mary Anne and I babysat for the Pikes. I'm really surprised that we were able to pull it off. Hereby let it be known that it is possible: 1) for two people to babysit for eight kids without losing their sanity (the sitters' or the kids'), and 2) for the babysitters to accomplish this without ever speaking to each other. There should be a Babysitters' Hall of Fame where experiences like ours could be recorded and preserved for all to read about. To do what we did takes a lot of imagination.

Kristy's wrong. Imagination isn't all it takes. It takes a good fight, too. You have to be pretty mad at a person in order even to think about doing what we did at the Pikes' that evening.

Before I go into what happened, though, let me say a little about the Pike kids. The most interesting thing is that three of the kids are triplets – Byron, Adam and Jordan – identical boys. (Kristy and I can tell them apart, though.) They're nine. The oldest Pike is Mallory, who's ten, and is usually a big help to babysitters. After the triplets come Vanessa, who's eight; Nicholas (Nicky), who's seven; and Margo and Claire, who are six and four. They're quite a brood. Actually, they're really good kids, but their parents have raised them liberally (according to my father), and without batting an eye, they do things I'd never *dream* of. For instance, Claire sometimes takes off her clothes and runs around the house naked. No one pays a bit of attention. After a while, she just puts her clothes back on. Also, although each of the kids has to be in bed at a specific time, none of them has to turn out the light and go to sleep until he or she feels like it. As long as they're in bed, they can stay up as late as they want. And they don't have to eat any food they don't like.

Kristy and I showed up at the Pikes' at five o'clock on Friday afternoon. We showed up separately, of course. Actually, I have to admit that I'd sort of been tailing Kristy all the way to the house. Since the Pikes don't live too far from Bradford Court, we were walking to their house, and I wasn't far behind Kristy. I had to go very quietly so she wouldn't know I was there. Once she turned around suddenly, and I had to duck behind a bush so she wouldn't see me. When we reached the Pikes', I hovered around the end of their driveway while Kristy went inside. I waited until the door had closed behind her. Then I rang the bell.

Mr and Mrs Pike were in a rush. Mrs Pike let me in hurriedly and she and her husband started giving Kristy and me instructions. They were gone almost before I knew it. As soon as they left, the kids surrounded Kristy and me. They like babysitters.

"What's for dinner?" asked Byron, whose hobby is eating.

"Cold fried chicken or tuna sandwiches," Kristy replied.

"Can I have both?"

"No," Kristy said.

"Yes," I said.

"I don't like chicken *or* tuna fish," Margo complained.

"Then make yourself a peanut butter sandwich," suggested Mallory.

"OK," agreed Margo.

"When do we eat?" asked Byron.

"Six o'clock," I answered.

"Six-thirty," said Kristy.

"Can I watch cartoons?" asked Claire.

"Can we make an obstacle course in the living room?" asked Jordan, speaking for the triplets.

"Can I just read?" asked Vanessa, who's quiet. "I'm in the middle of *The Phantom Tollbooth*."

"Can I colour?" asked Margo.

"Can we start a baseball game?" asked Nicky.

"Can I help make dinner?" asked Mallory.

"Yes, no, yes, yes, no, and yes," I replied.

The kids laughed. Kristy scowled.

"Let's do something together," said Adam. "There are ten people. We could do something with teams, five on a team."

"Hey, Kristy," I said, suddenly inspired. "How about putting on a play?"

Kristy pretended not to hear me.

It was my turn to scowl.

"Mallory," I said, "tell Kristy it would be fun to put on a play."

"Kristy," Mallory began, "Mary Anne says— Hey, how come she didn't hear you, Mary Anne? She's not deaf."

"I know." I tried to think of a way to explain what was going on. "We're . . . we're playing Telephone."

"We are? Then wait. OK, everybody," Mallory said to her brothers and sisters. "Let's sit down in a line, right here in the living room. And Kristy, you sit at that end, and Mary Anne, you sit at the other end. Now, start the game, Mary Anne."

Just for fun, I leaned over to Adam, who was next to me, and whispered, "Kristy Thomas is a nosy, bossy busybody."

Adam giggled. Then he whispered to Jordan, Jordan whispered to Claire, and the game was under way.

By the time the message reached Kristy, she looked puzzled.

"What?" said Mallory. "What did you hear?"

"I heard, 'Cranky Tommy's nose is a bossy, busy boy.'"

The Pike kids laughed hysterically.

"OK, Mary Anne, now tell us what you really said," cried Mallory.

What I *really* said? I'd forgotten I'd have to do that. There was no way I could tell what I'd really said. I thought for a moment. "I said, 'Crystal tambourines—'"

"No, you didn't," interrupted Adam. "You said 'Critical' – I mean 'Christopher' – I mean . . . Oh, I don't know what you said!"

Everyone was laughing again. "Kristy, you start one this time," I suggested.

Kristy ignored me.

Oh, brother.

I whispered to Adam, "Tell Kristy to start the game."

By the time the message reached Kristy, she said, "Tired carrots take the blame?"

"No, *start* the *game!*" shouted Adam.

We played a while longer, letting different kids take turns being on the ends. Luckily, Kristy and I never had to sit next to each other.

Promptly at six o'clock, Byron looked at his watch and announced, "It's time for dinner! Let's eat!"

"OK," replied Kristy. "Into the kitchen, everybody!" She seemed to have forgotten that she'd said dinner was at six-thirty.

I could see that she planned to take charge.

"Wash your hands," I told the kids.

"No, we don't have to," said Nicky.

"Not unless we want to," added Margo.

Kristy smirked at me.

In the kitchen, pandemonium broke out. Ten people were scrambling around, getting out plates, forks, spoons and glasses, and pulling food out of the refrigerator.

Kristy stuck her fingers in her mouth and whistled shrilly.

Silence.

"Now hold it!" said Kristy.

"We need some order," I added.

"What?" said Kristy. "Did somebody say something?"

"She said we need order," replied Mallory.

"We need order," Adam told Byron.

"We need order," Byron told Jordan.

"We need order," Jordan told Vanessa.

"We need order," Vanessa told Nicky.

"We need order," Nicky told Margo.

"We need order," Margo told Claire.

Claire hugged Kristy around the knees and grinned up at her. "We need order, Kristy," she said. "Whatever that is."

Kristy actually smiled. "Tell Margo to sit down."

"Sit down," said Claire, finding her place at the long table in the kitchen.

Margo sat. "Sit down," she told Nicky.

Nicky sat. "Sit down," he told Vanessa.

Vanessa sat. "Sit down," she told Jordan.

Jordan sat. "Sit down," he told Byron.

Byron was already sitting down, waiting for food to appear in front of him. "I am sitting," he said. "Sit down," he told Adam.

Adam sat. "Sit down," he told Mallory.

Mallory sat. "Sit down," she told me.

"No," I said, smiling. "*I* am going to serve you guys."

And that's how the rest of dinner went. Not once did Kristy and I have to speak to each other, and the Pike kids never realized anything was wrong. They thought we were playing a great game, and I could tell they were probably going to play it themselves for a long time. I felt slightly sorry for their parents.

By the time we finished dinner, it was after seven o'clock. The meal had taken an unusually long time because every word of conversation had to be repeated nine times and go all the way around the table, with much giggling. I finally put an end to the meal when Nicky, who was sitting between Claire and Jordan, turned to Jordan and said, "Tell Claire she's a hot-dog-head."

"Claire, you're a hot-dog-head," Jordan told Vanessa.

"Claire, you're a hot-dog-head," Vanessa told Adam.

By the time the sentence reached Claire and she said to herself, "Claire, you're a hot-dog-head," Nicky laughed so hard he spit his milk across the table.

"OK, guys," I said. "Dinner's over. Help us clean up and put the dishes in the washer, and then we'll go do something."

"Do what?" asked Mallory.

"Put on a play," I said firmly, not bothering to look at Kristy. I didn't care whether she wanted to or not, and I didn't want the question asked ten times before I found out.

When the kitchen was clean (part of being a good babysitter is leaving a tidy house behind you), I gathered the kids and a reluctant Kristy downstairs in the playroom. "Now," I began, "we're going to put on—"

"—whatever you want," Kristy supplied.

I tried not to look as angry as I felt. I'd been planning on suggesting a Winnie-the-Pooh story because there were so many Pooh characters and I thought that even Claire and Margo would know some of the tales.

But at Kristy's words, everybody started shouting.

"The Phantom Tollbooth!" cried Vanessa.

"Spider-Man!" yelled Adam and Jordan.

"Peter Rabbit," suggested Claire.

After about ten minutes of arguing, we decided to put on two plays. Under Kristy's direction, the triplets and Mallory were going to put on a play called *Super-Girl Meets the Super-Nerds*. (A sound effects record was going to be involved.) Under my direction, Nicky, Vanessa, Claire and Margo were going to put on *Peter Rabbit*. I took them upstairs to rehearse in the living room.

The Pike kids had lots of fun with their plays, and by the time I looked at my watch again, it was eight-thirty. Yikes! It was time for Margo and Claire to be in bed, and time for Nicky and Vanessa to start getting ready for bed. Furthermore, if Mr and Mrs Pike weren't home in about twenty minutes, I wouldn't be home by nine. But they had promised, and they usually kept their promises.

I took Margo and Claire upstairs and put them to bed, while Nicky and Vanessa changed into their pyjamas. Kristy stayed downstairs with Mallory and the triplets. When the littlest ones were settled, I closed the door to their room gently.

"You guys want a story?" I asked Nicky and Vanessa.

"Yes! Yes! We're in the middle of *Pippi Longstocking*!"

So we read a few pages. I looked at my watch. Five minutes to nine! What was I going to do? If I left early, the Pikes would be upset. After all, they were paying for two sitters. If I got home late, Dad would be upset.

Luckily, just as I was starting to panic, I heard the Pikes arrive. I shooed Nicky and Vanessa into their bedrooms. "Your mom and dad will say goodnight to you in a few minutes," I assured them.

Then I dashed downstairs. There was no time for dignity. "Mrs Pike," I said breathlessly, not daring to look at Kristy, "I've got to be home *right now*! It's almost nine."

"I know, Mary Anne. I'm sorry we're late. We got caught in a traffic jam on the way back. Hop in the car with Mr Pike, you two," she told Kristy and me. "He'll give you a lift home. Oh, and he'll pay you when he drops you off."

"OK," I said. "Thanks. Bye!"

When Mr Pike let us off in front of our houses, it was five minutes after nine. He paid us a little extra, since they'd been on the late side, which was nice of him. Then he drove off. I sprinted for my front door. Just as I reached it, I heard Kristy call from the darkness, "Baby, baby, baby!"

Humiliated, I let myself inside.

My father was waiting for me.

Chapter 10

"Hi, Dad," I greeted him apprehensively.

"Mary Anne, I was just starting to worry."

"I'm sorry I'm late. The Pikes got stuck in a traffic jam. They couldn't help it. . . I couldn't help it."

"That's all right. It's only five minutes after nine. I know things come up."

I was so relieved he wasn't upset that I decided to bring up a touchy subject again. "You know, Dad," I began, "it would be a lot easier on my clients if I could babysit just a little later – say until ten. Or even nine-thirty. That would do."

"Mary Anne," Dad said gently, "we've been through that. If your clients need someone who can stay out late, then they should look for an older sitter."

"But Kristy and Claudia and Stacey—"

"I know. They're all allowed to stay out later, and they're the same age as you."

"Right."

"But they're not you. And their parents aren't me. I have to do what I think is best for you."

I nodded.

"And the next time it looks as though you're going to be late – for whatever reason – give me a call to let me know, all right?"

"OK."

Was Dad trying to tell me something? Was he saying that I hadn't been responsible? Maybe if I was more responsible, he'd let me stay out later. Maybe he made decisions based on responsibility, not age. It was something to think about.

I began thinking right away, on my way upstairs to bed. I felt that I was already fairly responsible. I always did my homework and I got good grades in school. I was usually on time for things. I usually started dinner for Dad and me. I did almost everything my father told me to do. Still . . . I supposed there was always room for more responsibility. I *could* have called Dad from the Pikes' instead of panicking. I could start facing up to things I was afraid of.

One of my biggest fears is confronting people and dealing with people I don't know – like picking up the phone to get information, or talking to sales clerks, or asking for directions. Dad knew all that. Maybe when I stopped avoiding things, he would notice.

Even though my father didn't know about the fight everyone in the Babysitters Club had had, I decided that it was really time to do something about it. Whether the fault was mine or somebody else's (or everybody's), I was going to fix things. Now *that* was taking on responsibility.

I realized that the evening at the Pikes' could have been a disaster. If the kids had noticed that Kristy and I were fighting, it would have looked bad for our club. Luckily for us, the Pike kids are easy-going and have a sense of humour.

Luckily.

What if one of the kids had gotten hurt, and Kristy and I hadn't been able to agree on what to do about it? What if the kids had realized what was going on? They might have blabbed to their parents, and our club might have lost some of its best clients.

Besides, trying to run a club without meetings was stupid.

It was time to put the club back together before it fell apart completely. Since Kristy is the club president, I thought that the best way to do it was to make up with her. That was going to be a real challenge. It would take plenty of responsibility.

How to make up with Kristy? Long after I'd turned out my light, I lay in bed thinking. I could try to write her a note – one I could actually send her:

> Dear Kristy,
> I'm really sorry about our fight. I'd like to make up and be friends again.
> Your best friend (I hope),
> Mary Anne

That was good. Short but sweet.

And it was truthful. I really was sorry about our fight, no matter who had started it or whose fault it was. And I really did want to be friends again.

The next morning was Saturday, but I woke up early anyway. I ate breakfast with my father. Then I went back to my room and wrote the note to Kristy.

And *then* – how was I going to get the note to her? If I took it over personally, she'd close the door in my face. Maybe I could leave it in the mailbox, or give it to David Michael to give to her.

No. How could I be sure she'd read it? Maybe a note wasn't a good idea. But I couldn't think of another way to make up with Kristy.

I was still stewing about it when I heard the phone ring. A few moments later, my father called up the stairs, "Mary Anne! It's for you!"

"OK!"

As I ran to the phone, one teensy little part of me thought it might be Kristy, calling to apologize to *me*.

No such luck. It was Dawn. But I was glad to hear from her.

"Hi!" I said.

"Hi! What are you doing today?"

"Nothing. What are you doing?"

"Nothing."

"Want to come over?"

"Sure! Right now?"

"Yeah. I don't know what we'll do, but we'll think of something."

"OK. I'll be right there."

"Good," I said. We hung up.

Dawn rode over on her bicycle, and she reached my house in record time.

I met her at the door and we ran up to my room. The first thing Dawn said was, "Mary Anne, I was thinking as I rode over here, and you know what we forgot to do?"

"What?" I asked.

"Find out if your father and my mother knew each other when they were young."

"Oh, that's right!" I exclaimed. "Did your mom go to Stoneybrook High?"

"Yup," replied Dawn. "Did your dad?"

"Yup! Oh, this is exciting!"

"What year did your father graduate?" Dawn asked.

"Gee," I said slowly, "I don't know."

"Well, how old is he?"

"Let's see. He's forty-one. . . No, he's forty-two. Forty-two. That's right."

"Really? So's my mom!"

"You're kidding! I bet they did know each other. Let's go ask my father."

We were racing down the hall and had just reached the head of the stairs when Dad appeared at the bottom. "Mary Anne," he said, "I've got to go into the office for several hours. I'll be back this afternoon. You may heat up that casserole for lunch. Dawn is welcome to stay, all right?"

"OK. Thanks, Dad. See you later."

Dawn nudged me with her elbow. I knew she wanted me to ask Dad about Mrs Schafer, but it wasn't the right time. Dad was in a hurry, and he doesn't like to be bothered with questions when he's rushing off somewhere. As soon as he left, Dawn said, slightly accusingly, "Why didn't you ask him?"

"It wasn't a good time. Believe me. Besides, I have another idea. His yearbooks are in the den. Let's go look at them. I used to go through them all the time when I was little, but I bet I haven't opened one since I was nine."

"Oh goody, yearbooks!" said Dawn.

In the den, we stood before a bookcase with a row of heavy old yearbooks in it. "Why are there so many?" asked Dawn.

"They're my mother's *and* my father's – high school and university. So there are sixteen in all. Now let's see. Here are the Stoneybrook High yearbooks. These are Dad's, since my mother grew up in Maryland. Which one should we look at first?"

"His senior yearbook," Dawn answered immediately. "It'll have the biggest pictures. What year is this? Oh, this is the year my mom graduated, too! So they were in the same class. I bet they did know each other."

Dawn pulled the book off the shelf, and I blew the dust from the cover. "Yuck," I said. We stopped for a moment to look at the book.

The year Dad had graduated was printed across the cover in large, white raised numbers.

We opened it gingerly, as if it would fall apart.

"Here are the seniors," said Dawn, turning to the front of the book. We peered at row after row of black-and-white photos, the students looking funny and old-fashioned. Under each picture was a little paragraph, words that meant nothing to Dawn and me. Inside jokes, I guessed. I wondered if the people who had composed them would know what they meant twenty-five years later. Under one boy's photo was written: "Thumpers . . . Apple Corps . . . Arnie and Gertrude . . . S.A.B." Under a girl's was written: "White Phantom Chevy . . . 'Broc' junior classroom . . . 'Rebel Rousers' & George." And one boy had written something that Dawn and I decided must be a code: E.S.R., A.T., DUDE, FIBES, G.F.R. . . ALRIGHT.

"He spelled 'all right' all wrong," Dawn remarked.

Then we started laughing. "Look at that girl's hair!" I shrieked. "It looks like she blew it up with a bicycle pump!"

Dawn rolled over on the floor, giggling. "Now let's find your dad," she said. The seniors were in alphabetical order. We flipped through until we reached the *S*'s.

"There he is!" I cried, jabbing at the picture in the upper left-hand corner of a page. "There he is! Oh, wow, I forgot how weird he looks! He doesn't look like my father at all. He looks . . . like an alien!"

"He was only seventeen, I guess, but somehow he looks a lot older," Dawn pointed out.

"He had a crew cut! Let's see what's under his picture. . . This is weird. It says: "To S.E.P.: Don't walk in front of me – I may not follow. Don't walk behind me – I may not lead. Walk beside me – and just be my friend. – Camus.' Who's Camus?" I asked.

"Beats me," Dawn replied, "but S.E.P. – those were my mother's initials before she got married."

Dawn and I looked at each other with wide eyes.

"Quick!" exclaimed Dawn. "Turn to the *P*'s! We're looking for Sharon Porter."

Frantically, we flipped the pages back.

"Stop! We're in the *M*'s!"

We went forward a few pages.

"There she is!" shouted Dawn. "Sharon Emerson Porter. That's all it says under her picture. Just her name. No quotes or silly stuff."

"But she signed Dad's yearbook," I said, looking at the scrawly message in blue ink that covered Sharon Porter's face.

We leaned over.

"'Dearest Richie,'" Dawn read.

"Richie!" I cried. "No one calls him *Richie*."

Mystified, Dawn read on. "'Four years weren't enough. Let's start over. How can we part? We have one more summer. Hold on to it, Richie. (Love is blind.) Always and for ever, Sharon.'"

"I guess they did know each other," said Dawn at last.

"I'll say," I said. "I'll say."

Chapter 11

Dawn and I practically suffered dual heart attacks after reading what was written in my dad's yearbook. We agreed not to mention our discovery to our parents, although we weren't sure why we wanted to keep the secret.

We spent the rest of the day hashing it over. Then on Sunday we went through Dawn's mother's yearbook. The book was hard to find, since it was still packed away. We finally located it at the bottom of a carton labelled KITCHEN.

"Kitchen?" I said to Dawn.

She shrugged. "Don't ask."

We opened the book, knowing exactly where to look. Written across my father's picture in round, familiar handwriting was, "For Sharon, who knows what this means." (An arrow pointed to the quote from the person named Camus.) "Remember – the summer can be for ever. Love always, Richie."

"People sure get poetic in high school," Dawn remarked. "What does 'the summer can be for ever' mean?"

I didn't know. But far more interesting than what Dad had written was what was pressed between the "S" pages of Dawn's mother's book. It was a rose, brown and dried, with a stained, yellowing ribbon tied to the stem.

Although I had vowed to find a way to get the Babysitters Club back together, things kept coming up to take my mind off of it. First, of course, was the discovery about Dawn's mother and my father. Dawn and I talked about it all week. We had a million questions, and we could only guess at the answers to them.

"What do you think the rose is from?" asked Dawn.

"A prom?" I suggested. "I bet they went to their senior prom together. I wonder what they wore."

"Hey," said Dawn. She crunched loudly on a piece of celery. Dawn refused to buy the school lunches, saying they were starchy and gross. As soon as her mother had got their kitchen in order, Dawn had insisted on bringing her own healthy lunches to school each day. "Don't parents *always* take pictures of their kids just before they go off to their proms?" she asked. "I mean, even back in those days, it was like a rule of parenthood. Your daughter's date arrives to take her to the prom. He's wearing a tux and your daughter is wearing her new gown and carrying a shawl. Then the parents *have* to make them pose in front of the mantelpiece in the living room for the ceremonial prom pictures, which they send to the relatives and to the boy's family."

I giggled. "But what does that have to do with our parents?"

"Well, there must be a prom picture of them somewhere. If we could find a picture, we could see if my mother was wearing a rose with a satin ribbon tied to it."

"Oh! Great idea," I said. But we couldn't find any prom pictures.

Another day we tried to guess what their notes to each other meant.

"'Just one more summer,'" I repeated sadly. "I wonder why they knew they would have to break up at the end of the summer. Or maybe that's not what they meant at all."

"It must be what they meant. But why?"

"I don't know."

"I wonder what your mother meant by 'love is

blind,'" I said to Dawn on Friday.

"Maybe someone disapproved of their relationship, but my mom and your dad were too much in love to see what was wrong."

"But what could have been wrong?"

"I don't know," Dawn replied. "But I bet someone disapproved of them."

"But we don't know for sure," I pointed out.

"No, that's true."

On Saturday, something else happened to keep my mind off the club. It was what turned out to be my scariest babysitting experience ever. Earlier in the week, Mrs Prezzioso had called needing a babysitter for Jenny all Saturday afternoon. Even though the Prezziosos are weird, I sort of like Jenny. So I took the job.

I arrived at the Prezziosos' house promptly at eleven-thirty. I rang the bell.

A few moments later I could hear little feet run to the door. Then I heard the locks being turned. "Hey, Jenny!" I called. "Ask who it is first."

"Oh, yeah," I heard her say. "Who is it?"

"It's me, Mary Anne Spier, your babysitter."

"Are you a stranger?"

I sighed. "No. I'm Mary Anne. You know me."

The door was opened.

"Hi, Mary Anne," said Jenny. She was wearing

113

a pale blue dress with a white collar and cuffs. Her tights were white. Her shoes were white. Her hair ribbon was white. I could tell it was going to be a long day.

Jenny's mother appeared behind her. "Well," began Mrs Prezzioso, smoothing away a non-existent wrinkle in her black silk cocktail dress, "Mr Prezzioso and I are going to be up in Chatham for a basketball game." (Mrs P. was wearing a cocktail dress to a basketball game?) "My husband's college is playing their biggest rival. It's some sort of important championship or something. He's very excited about it, so we're going to drive up there, meet some friends, go to the game, and go out for an early dinner. We should be home by seven at the very latest.

"I'm a bit nervous, though, about being so far away," she added. (Chatham is an hour north of Stoneybrook.)

"I'm sure everything will be fine," I said.

"Well, I've left you a lot of phone numbers – our phones, Jenny's doctor, the number of the gymnasium where the game will be held, our next-door neighbours, and the usual emergency numbers."

"OK," I said. I realized Jenny was being awfully

quiet. I wondered what she had up her sleeve.

But I didn't have much time to dwell on it. At that moment, Mr P. ran down the stairs. He was wearing blue jeans and a striped polo shirt. I was willing to bet that there had been some battle over his clothing that morning. Maybe that was why Jenny was so quiet.

I looked at her. She was sitting in an armchair in the living room, her legs sticking out in front of her, her head leaning back listlessly. She appeared to be listening to us.

I noticed that Mrs P. did not stand next to her husband and ask me how they looked. Frankly, I couldn't blame Mr P. for dressing the way he did, but I was sorry if it had caused a fight that had upset Jenny.

At last, after lots more instructions and cautions, the Prezziosos left. Jenny didn't even bother to wave goodbye to them.

"Well," I said to her, "what do you want to do today? We've got the whole afternoon to play."

Jenny stuck out her lower lip. "Nothing."

"You don't want to do anything?"

She crossed her arms. "No."

"Hey, come on. It's not that cold out. You want to see if Claire Pike can play?"

"NONONONONO!"

For such a little kid, Jenny certainly has a big set of lungs.

"OK, OK," I said. What a fusspot. "I brought the Kid-Kit," I told her a few moments later.

"I know. I saw."

What she didn't know was that there was nothing even remotely messy in it. The paint-with-water book was at home on my bed.

I decided to try one more thing. "Do you want to read a story?"

Jenny shrugged. "I guess."

At last. That was a relief. I took *Blueberries for Sal*, *The Tale of Squirrel Nutkin*, and *Caps for Sale* out of the Kid-Kit. "Which one?" I asked.

Jenny shrugged.

I chose *Blueberries for Sal*. "Come sit by me on the sofa." Wordlessly, Jenny got up, climbed on to the sofa, and leaned against me. I began to read. When I reached the part of the story that I thought was the most exciting, Jenny didn't even make a sound. I glanced at her. She was sound asleep.

That's strange, I thought. Mrs P. had told me Jenny had slept late that morning and probably wouldn't take her afternoon nap. Yet there she was, asleep at twelve noon.

I eased myself up and laid Jenny on the sofa.

116

That was when I realized how warm she was. I put my hand on her forehead.

She was burning up.

I shook her gently. "Jenny! Jenny!"

"Mmphh," she mumbled. She stirred but didn't wake up.

My heart pounding, I raced upstairs to the bathroom off of Jenny's parents' bedroom and looked frantically through the medicine cabinet. When I found a thermometer, I dashed downstairs with it.

Even though Jenny was still asleep, I stuck it under her tongue. I sat there until the thermometer beeped, then removed it and peered at the numbers.

Forty degrees!

Forty. I'd never had a fever that high.

I began making phone calls.

First I tried Mr P's and Mrs P's phones. No one answered. I left messages.

Next I called Jenny's doctor and got his answering service. A bored-sounding woman said the doctor would call back when he could.

That might not be fast enough. I called the Pikes. No answer.

I called the next-door neighbours. No answer.

I called my dad, even though I knew he was

out shopping and rarely remembered to turn his phone on. No answer.

What to do? I didn't dare call the other members of the Babysitters Club, so at last I called Dawn.

"I'll be right there," she told me.

While I waited for her, I called the gym in Chatham and left an urgent message for the Prezziosos to be paged as soon as possible and told to call home. I knew they hadn't reached the gym yet.

When Dawn arrived, I showed her Jenny sleeping on the sofa, and told her the people I'd tried to reach.

"And the doctor hasn't called back yet?" she asked.

I shook my head. "I guess we could just call for an ambulance, but really, she's only got a fever. I mean, it's not like she broke her leg or something."

"I know," said Dawn. "If Mom were home, she could drive us to the emergency room, but she took my brother out to Washington Mall. Hey, try calling nine-nine-nine. Maybe someone could tell us what to do. At least they'd know whether it would be all right to call for an ambulance."

"OK," I agreed.

Dawn sat with Jenny while I made the call.

A man answered the phone, sounding calm and pleasant.

"Hi," I said. "I'm babysitting for a three-year-old and she fell asleep and I realized she has a fever and it's forty degrees. And," I rushed on, "I can't reach her parents or my dad or the neighbours, and I called her doctor but all I got was the answering service and he hasn't called back yet and I'm really worried."

"All right. Try to relax a little," the man said. "Young children often run fevers and it turns out to be just a sign of a simple infection. Sometimes it's nothing at all. However, forty is high and she should be looked at right away. I think the best thing to do is to get her to the emergency room of the hospital."

"But I'm only twelve," I said. "I can't drive."

"And you've tried reaching the neighbours?"

"Yes, several of them. And my dad."

"Well, then, I'll send an ambulance around."

"You *will*?" I said.

"Just tell me the address."

I gave it to him. Then he instructed me to get Jenny ready to leave the house and to keep cold compresses on her forehead until the ambulance arrived. I thanked him and we hung up.

"OK, Dawn," I said, running into the living

room. "An ambulance is on the way. I spoke to a man, and he said to get Jenny ready to leave and to keep cold compresses on her head until the ambulance gets here."

"I'll make a compress, you get her coat," said Dawn.

Dawn dashed into the kitchen, while I found Jenny's coat and mittens in the closet. I laid them next to her on the sofa, but didn't put them on her. I didn't want to make her hotter than she already was.

Dawn returned with a cold compress made from a tea towel. I held it to Jenny's forehead. "Oh, you know what?" I said. "Can you leave a message on the Prezziosos' phones and tell them where we're going? And also call the Lewiston Gymnasium in Chatham again and leave a message for the Prezziosos to turn around as soon as they reach the gym, and go right to the emergency room of the hospital here. I just left a message for them to call home, but if they do, no one will answer the phone."

"OK." Dawn dashed off, then returned and stood looking out of the front window. "Try to wake Jenny up," she said several moments later. "The ambulance is coming."

"OK. . . Come on, Jenny-bunny," I said. I shook

her shoulder and sat her up. She fell to the side like a limp rag doll. "Nap time's over. Wake up."

Jenny opened her eyes a crack. "No," she said sleepily.

"Sorry, Jenny. I know you're not feeling well, so you have to see the doctor."

That woke her up – a little. "The doctor?" she repeated.

"Yup. He'll make you feel better. Come on, I want you to put your coat on."

Jenny allowed me to slip her coat and mittens on while Dawn let the ambulance attendants in. They were wheeling a stretcher through the front door.

"That the little girl?" asked one man, pointing to Jenny.

"Yes," I replied, "and she has a high fever, but she's not hurt. I don't think you need the stretcher."

They agreed. Dawn grabbed her jacket and mine as the man picked Jenny up gently and carried her out to the ambulance. I ran along behind him. "Lock the front door!" I called over my shoulder to Dawn as she dashed out with our jackets.

The attendants settled the still-sleepy Jenny in the ambulance, and I rode in back with her while Dawn rode up front next to the driver. I'd never been in an ambulance before, but I was too concerned about Jenny to be nervous.

As we zipped along (no siren or lights, but plenty of speed) the attendants took Jenny's temperature (steady at forty), checked her pulse and blood pressure, listened to her heart, and looked at her ears. The man attendant kept talking to her and asking her questions. I looked at him, puzzled.

"Just trying to keep her awake," he told me.

I nodded.

We reached Stoneybrook General Hospital and pulled up to the entrance to the emergency room. One of the attendants carried Jenny inside, Dawn and I following, and spoke to a nurse. The nurse hustled us into a little curtained-off room. Then the attendant left and the nurse, clipboard in hand, started asking questions about Jenny. I answered them as well as I could. "Her parents will be here later, and they can fill you in," I told her finally.

She nodded. "A doctor will look in on her as soon as possible," she said. Then she parted the curtain and walked briskly down the hallway. A few moments later she returned with a cold compress, then disappeared again.

Dawn and I looked at each other. "Now what?" asked Dawn.

"Now we wait, I guess." I adjusted the compress on Jenny's forehead. "How are you feeling?" I asked her. She seemed a bit more alert, but as hot as ever.

"Hot," she replied. "And my throat hurts. And my head."

"Yuck," I said. "I'm sorry. The doctor will be here soon, though, and he'll help you feel better. He or she, I mean."

"Look what I brought," Dawn spoke up.

"Hey, who's that?" asked Jenny, finally noticing her visitor.

"That's my friend Dawn. Dawn Schafer."

"Hi, Jenny," said Dawn.

"Hi. . . What did you bring?"

"This." Dawn held up *Blueberries for Sal*.

"Oh goody," said Jenny.

I began to read. We were halfway through the story when a doctor poked her head through the curtain.

"Jenny Prezzioso?" she asked.

"That's Jenny," I said, pointing. "I'm Mary Anne Spier, her babysitter."

"Well, let's see what we have here."

The doctor examined Jenny gently.

123

"It looks like a nice case of strep throat," she said after a while. "I want to draw some blood and do a throat culture to be sure, but I don't think it's anything more serious than that. . . Where are her parents?"

I explained. Then I looked at my watch. "If her parents got their messages already, they could be at the hospital in half an hour to forty-five minutes."

The doctor nodded. "Well, she can stay here until her parents arrive. While we're running the tests, I'll have a nurse try to bring her fever down. I'd like to talk to the Prezziosos before Jenny leaves."

"OK," I said.

A nurse entered. She drew some blood from Jenny, which made her cry, and took a throat culture, which made her gag. But when she began bathing her in alcohol, Jenny said, "Oh, that feels good."

Her temperature dropped a degree and a half.

By the time the Prezziosos arrived, Jenny was on the verge of a temper tantrum. I took it as a good sign.

Chapter 12

Mrs Prezzioso was nearly hysterical. She flew into Jenny's cubicle in the emergency room, sobbing loudly, then hugged Jenny to her, pressing Jenny's face against her cocktail dress. "Oh, my baby!" she cried. "Angel, how are you feeling?"

"I feel better, Mommy," Jenny said. "Nice and cool."

Her temperature was still thirty-eight degrees. I could only imagine how Jenny had felt when it was forty degrees.

The doctor returned and spoke briefly to the Prezziosos, assuring them that Jenny was already on the mend. "I want to give you a prescription and make an appointment to see her again on Monday," she added. "And I need you to fill out some forms."

"Why don't you take care of that, dear," Mr Prezzioso said to his wife, "while I take Mary

Anne and Dawn home? Then I'll come back for you and our angel."

Mrs P. agreed, so Dawn and I said goodbye to the angel and her mother, and followed Mr P. out to his car.

"Actually, we need to go back to your house," I told him. "I left some things in the living room, and Dawn's bicycle is there."

"All right," he said.

On the way to the Prezziosos', Mr P. told Dawn and me over and over what a wonderful job we had done, and how proud of us he was.

"I hope you don't mind that I called a friend," I said apprehensively. "I really needed help, and I couldn't reach the neighbours or my dad."

"Or my mother," added Dawn.

"Not at all," said Mr P. "You did just the right thing. I can't believe our phones were off. Leaving a message at the gym was smart. Apparently, they started paging us right away and just kept paging until we arrived. The first thing we heard when we entered the gym was our names being called over the tannoy. . . How did you get Jenny to the hospital?"

"I called nine-nine-nine and told the man I talked to how high Jenny's temperature was and said we couldn't find anyone to drive us to the hospital. He sent an ambulance over. . . Oh, and Jenny's doctor is probably going to call you back today. He was the first person I called, and I left a message with his service. He hadn't called back by the time we left for the hospital."

Again Mr P. looked impressed. "Thanks, Mary Anne," he said. "You, too, Dawn. I want you to know that I'll always feel at ease having Jenny in your competent hands."

Wow, I thought. Our competent hands. That was a real compliment.

When Dawn had gotten her bicycle from the Prezziosos' driveway and I had retrieved the Kid-Kit from the living room, Mr P. paid Dawn and me twice what he owed – *each*. "For a job well done," he said.

"Thanks!" I exclaimed. "Thanks a lot!"

"Yeah," said Dawn. "You really didn't have to pay me."

"I know," said Mr P., "but you deserve it." He headed back to the hospital.

"Want to come over for a while?" I asked Dawn. The day had turned grey and drizzly. I thought we could spend the rest of the afternoon fooling around in my room. I had found two more old photo albums in the den, and through incredible will power, had managed not to peek at them until Dawn was with me.

"Sure," said Dawn. "Just remind me to call my mom and tell her where I am."

Dawn rode slowly over to my house, and I trotted along next to her. I let us in the front door and called for my father, but he wasn't home yet. Then Dawn phoned her mother, who also wasn't home yet, and left a message for her on their answering machine.

"Are you hungry?" I asked. I had just realized that, with the excitement over, I was starving.

"Famished," replied Dawn.

We made sandwiches and ate them in the kitchen, discussing our adventure. "Isn't Mrs P. weird?" I said. "Did you see her fancy black dress? That's what she was wearing to a basketball game!"

"And she calls Jenny her angel."

I giggled. "Yeah. Mr P. does, too. But he's all right. I like him."

"He's generous," added Dawn. "Gosh, this is a lot of money."

When we were finished with lunch, I said, "Let's go upstairs. I want to show you something."

We ran up to my room and, with a flourish, I pulled the two old photo albums out from under my bed. "We haven't looked through these," I told Dawn. "I have no idea what's in them, but maybe we'll find prom pictures."

"Yeah!"

We sat side by side on my bed and opened one of the heavy albums. It was so big it spread across both of our laps.

"These pictures look *old*," Dawn said.

"Yeah, really," I agreed. They were yellowed with age. Not one face was familiar. "I don't recognize any of these people," I said.

"You know what would be funny? If these weren't your family's albums at all. If there'd been some kind of mix-up and they were, like, Joe Schmoe's albums, and we spent all afternoon trying to find pictures of our parents among the Schmoe family."

I threw my head back and laughed. And as I lowered my head, I looked straight in front of me – out of my window and into Kristy's.

Kristy was staring back at me.

Since the day was dark, the overhead lights were on in our rooms and I knew that she had a perfect view of Dawn and me sitting side by side on my bed, laughing.

Kristy looked furious. (Good, she was jealous.) But she also looked . . . hurt? Or maybe betrayed.

I couldn't tell. For some mean reason, though, I felt triumphant. I'd show Kristy. I was no longer the old Mary Anne who depended on her for friendship and who went along with anything she said or did. I could take care of myself. I could make my own friends.

To be certain that she got the point, I put my arm around Dawn's shoulders. Then I stuck my tongue out at Kristy.

Kristy stuck her tongue out at me.

And Dawn looked up from the album just in time to see me with my tongue out. "Mary Anne, what—" she started to say. Then she followed my gaze out of the window and across to Kristy in her window.

She looked from me to Kristy and back to me again. "Who is that and what are you doing?" she asked.

Kristy crossed her eyes at us, then yanked her window shade down.

"What's going on?" Dawn demanded. "That girl looks familiar. I've seen her around school, haven't I?"

"Oh, that's just Kristy Thomas. She's nobody."

Dawn looked sceptical. "If she's nobody, how come you guys are bothering to stick your tongues out at each other?"

I took a deep breath, but before I could say anything, Dawn went on, "And how come you put your arm around me just now? Was that something you wanted Kristy to see?"

"Well, the thing is," I began, "Kristy and I *used* to be friends." (The truth was going to have to come out sometime.)

"And you had a fight, right?" asked Dawn. She put the album aside and got to her feet.

"Yes. . ."

"Mary Anne, the first day we met – when we were eating in the canteen – you told me you were sitting alone because your friends were all absent. Was Kristy one of those friends?"

"Yeah. . ."

"And then you kept on saying your friends were absent," Dawn continued thoughtfully. "It seemed kind of weird, but I needed a friend of my own so much, I guess I just tried to forget about your other friends. How come you said they were absent?"

"Well, see, we'd just had this big fight, and we were all mad at each other. . ." I trailed off.

Dawn nodded her head. She looked really disgusted. "So you lied to me," she said.

"I guess," I replied uncomfortably.

"From the first day of our friendship you lied to me."

I didn't know what to say to that.

"You know, not bothering to tell a person the real truth," Dawn went on, "is just as bad as telling lies. You've been lying to me the whole time we were friends, you know that?"

"Hey, that is not true!" I cried, jumping up.

"Why should I believe that, coming from a liar? I'll tell you what I do believe, though. I believe I was pretty convenient when you needed a new friend. . . No, don't say anything, Mary Anne," she rushed on when I started to protest. "I know the rest of *this* story. See you later." Dawn stomped down the stairs.

I jumped up and ran after her. "Watch those steps," I said sarcastically. "Hope you have a nice *trip*."

"Have a nice *life*," Dawn shouted over her shoulder. She let herself out the front door. I ran back to my room and stood at the window that faced the front of the house.

I watched my last friend pedal her bicycle furiously down the street.

Then I flung myself on my bed and cried.

Chapter 13

I spent the rest of the afternoon moping around my bedroom. My father called to say that he'd stopped in at the office, wouldn't be home until six, and could I please start dinner?

I did, numbly.

When Dad came home, we sat down to hamburgers, peas and French fries. Dad tried hard to make conversation, but I just didn't feel like talking. We were both relieved when the phone rang.

"I'll get it," said Dad. "I think it's a client." He reached behind him and picked up the phone. "Hello, Richard Spier. . . Pardon me? What antibiotics? . . . Oh, really? . . . No. No, she didn't. . . Well, I'm flattered to hear that. I'm proud of her, too. . . I'll give her the good news." Dad raised his eyebrows at me.

"What?" I mouthed.

He shook his head, meaning *I'll tell you in*

a minute. "Yes. I certainly will," he said. "All right . . . Thank you very much. Goodbye."

Dad hung up the phone, looking somewhat puzzled. "Mary Anne?" he asked. "Did any-thing . . . out of the ordinary happen today?"

I was so upset over my fight with Dawn (which was pretty out of the ordinary) that it was all I could think about. How could Dad possibly have heard about it, though? That couldn't have been Mrs Schafer on the phone. Dad had said he was proud of me. (He *had* meant me, hadn't he?)

Then in a flash I remembered Jenny Prezzioso. The trip to the hospital seemed like a million years ago. "Oh, my gosh!" I said. "How could I have forgotten to tell you? Yes, I— Who was that on the phone?"

"Mrs Prezzioso. She was calling to tell me what a good job you did this afternoon, and to let you know that Jenny does in fact have strep throat but is feeling much better. I was a little embarrassed to admit that I didn't know what she was talking about. I still don't think I know the whole story. Mrs Prezzioso was speaking very fast. She kept mentioning an angel."

I smiled. "That's Jenny. The Prezziosos call her their angel."

"Well, tell me what happened. It sounds rather exciting."

"It was, I guess, only I was so concerned about Jenny I hardly had time to feel excited or scared or anything. What happened was I was baby-sitting, and I noticed that Jenny seemed cranky and quiet, but at first I didn't think much of it. She gets cranky a lot. Then she fell asleep right in the middle of reading a book, and I realized she felt awfully warm, so I took her temperature. And, Dad, it was forty!"

"*Forty!*"

"Yes. I couldn't believe it, either. So I called her doctor, but I only got his answering service. Then I started calling neighbours, trying to find someone who could drive us to the doctor or the hospital, but no one was home—"

"Including me," added Dad.

"Including you. And including Dawn's mother. But Dawn came over, and she suggested dialling nine-nine-nine, so I did, and I explained everything to the man who answered, and he sent an ambulance over.

"You know," I went on, "now that I think about this afternoon, I'm surprised at everything I remembered to do. I remembered to call the gym in Chatham that the Prezziosos were driving to, so they could be paged to come home; I remembered all the instructions the man told me over the phone; and I remembered to lock the Prezziosos' front door as we left with the ambulance attendants."

Dad smiled at me. "Mrs Prezzioso said she was proud of you."

"So did her husband," I added.

"And so am I," said Dad.

"You are?"

"Very."

"Thanks," I said.

Dad sighed.

"What is it?"

"You're growing up," he said, as if it was some sort of revelation to him. "Right before my eyes."

"Well, I *am* twelve."

"I know. But twelve means different things for different people. It's like clothes. You can put a certain shirt on one person and he looks fabulous. Then you put the shirt on someone else and that person looks awful. It's the same way with age. It depends on how you wear it or carry it."

"You mean some twelve-year-olds are ready to date, and other twelve-year-olds still need babysitters?"

"Exactly."

"But isn't that a double standard?" I asked.

"No, just the opposite. An example of a double standard would be that just because a boy or girl had turned fourteen he or she would automatically be encouraged to date, no matter how mature he or she was – but absolutely no thirteen-year-old would be encouraged to do so."

"Oh. . . Am I. . ." I hardly dared to ask the question. "Am I more mature than you realized?"

"Yes. Yes, I think you are, Mary Anne."

"Am I . . ." (Oh, please, please, *please* let him say yes.) ". . . old enough to stay out a little later when I babysit?"

For a moment, Dad didn't answer. At last he said, "Well, ten o'clock seems a bit late for school nights. How about nine-thirty on school nights and ten o'clock on Friday and Saturday nights?"

"Oh, Dad, that's perfect! Thank you!" I started to get up, wanting to hug him, but we're not huggers. I sat down again. Then I had a great idea. "Dad, I want to show you something," I said. "I'll be right back." I ran upstairs to my room, pulled the rubber bands off the ends of my plaits, shook my hair out, and brushed it carefully. It fell over my shoulders, ripply from having been

137

braided when it was still damp that morning. Then I ran down to the kitchen and stood in front of my father. "How do I look?" I asked.

I watched Dad's face go from serious to soft. "Lovely," he finally managed to say.

"Do you think I could wear it this way? I mean just sometimes, not every day."

Dad nodded.

"And maybe," I went on, hoping I wasn't pressing my luck, "I could take Humpty Dumpty off my wall and put up a nice picture of Paris or New York instead?" I could ask him about Alice in Wonderland some other time.

Dad nodded. Then he held his arms out. I crossed the room to him and he folded me into his arms.

"Thank you, Dad," I said.

Before I went to bed that night, I wrote two letters, one to Kristy and one to Dawn. Both were apologies.

Chapter 14

Monday, February 9
The members of the Babysitters Club have been enemies for almost a month now. I can't believe it. Claudia, Kristy and Mary Anne – I hope you all read what I'm writing, because I think our fight is dumb, and you should know that. I thought you guys were my friends, but I guess not. I'm writing this because tomorrow the four of us have to help out at Jamie Newton's birthday party, and I think it's going to be a disaster. I hope you read this before then because I think you should be prepared for the worst.

P.S. If anybody wants to make up, I'm ready.

As it turned out, Stacey was both right and wrong. Jamie's party was *almost* a disaster, but something really good came out of it. I'm getting ahead of myself, though. Let me go back to Monday, the morning of the day Stacey wrote in our club notebook.

When I got to school, the first thing I did was find Dawn. I gave her the letter and stood next to her in the hall while she read it. I had been very honest in the letter, explaining that several times I *had* used her to make Kristy mad, but that I really liked her, and thought she was one of my best friends, Kristy or no Kristy. Then I apologized.

Dawn read the letter slowly. Then she read it again. Then she hugged me. I knew our fight was over.

A moment later, I realized that Dawn was staring at me. "What?" I asked.

"Mary Anne, your hair. . . Where are your plaits?"

I grinned. "Do you like it?"

"I love it! You look so pretty with your hair

140

down!" Dawn made me turn around so she could see me from the back, too.

"Thanks. I plan to wear it this way often." I opened my locker, put my lunch away, pulled out some books and slammed the locker shut again. "Now," I went on, "since I was able to make up with you, I ought to be able to make up with Kristy, too." I held up the other note I'd written. "This is for Kristy. I have to go find her."

I looked everywhere, but I couldn't find her. At last, just before the bell rang, I slipped the note into her locker. Several times that day I glimpsed her in the halls, and I knew she saw me, too, but she didn't say anything, and didn't act any differently than she had over the past few weeks.

Had she got the note? Maybe I'd stuck it in the wrong locker. Or maybe it had slid into a notebook and she hadn't seen it.

Or maybe she was just still mad.

Jamie's birthday party began at three-thirty that afternoon. I went to it with mixed feelings – excitement and dread. It could be a lot of fun. Or, as Stacey had pointed out, it could be a disaster. But the members of the Babysitters Club had promised Mrs Newton we'd help out, so I knew we'd all be there.

I rang the Newtons' bell at three-fifteen, armed with a present for Jamie. I had arrived early so I could give Mrs Newton a hand.

"Hi-hi!" Jamie greeted me excitedly. "I'm four today! Four years old! That's this many." He held up four fingers.

"Hi, Mary Anne," Mrs Newton called from the kitchen when Jamie let me in. "I'm glad you're here early. I can really use you." She put me to work filling goody baskets for the table and making punch. By the time I finished, most of Jamie's guests had arrived.

The living room sounded like a school playground. Jamie's friends, all dressed up in their party clothes, were running around, screaming and shrieking, and wanting him to open his presents. Mrs Newton pulled Kristy, Claudia, Stacey and me aside.

"Try to get them to sit down. We'll do presents first, because nobody can wait. It should go pretty fast."

The members of the Babysitters Club nodded. But we carefully avoided one another's eyes.

Mrs Newton clapped her hands. "Time for the presents!" she called.

Kristy rounded up four children and led them

to the sofa. "Sit over here," she told them.

Stacey rounded up four other children and led them to the floor in front of the fireplace.

Claudia guided several little girls to the floor by the piano.

Uh-oh, I thought. "Get everybody in one spot!" I directed.

Claudia, Stacey and Kristy gave me the evil eye.

"Around the couch is fine," said Mrs Newton.

Kristy gloated.

After Jamie had opened his presents, Mrs Newton announced that it was time for Pin the Tail on the Donkey. "Will three of you give me a hand, and somebody else go check on the baby?" Mrs Newton asked us.

The four of us made a mad dash for the stairs.

"*I'll* check on Lucy," said Kristy.

"No, *I* will," said Stacey.

"No, you won't. *I* will," I said.

"None of you will because *I'm* going!" Claudia exclaimed.

The four of us shoved one another around, trying to be the first to run up the stairs.

"Girls!" cried Mrs Newton.

We turned around guiltily. She was frowning at us.

"Stacey, would you please check on her?" said Mrs Newton. "I need the rest of you over here."

It was Stacey's turn to gloat. "Ha-ha," she said under her breath, and started up the staircase.

"Brat," muttered Kristy as we turned around.

Mrs Newton gave me the job of blindfolding the kids; Kristy, the job of guiding them if they strayed too far from the donkey; and Claudia, the job of watching the kids who were waiting their turn. Mrs Newton disappeared into the kitchen.

She hadn't been gone long when, just as I was tying the blindfold on Claire Pike, I felt something crunch down on my foot.

"Ow!" I cried.

"Oh, I'm *so* sorry!" I heard a voice say. "Was that your *foot* I stepped on?"

I straightened up and looked into Kristy's eyes. I narrowed my own eyes at her. "Yes, it was, Kristin Amanda Thomas," I said coldly. "Do you have a problem?"

"Yes, I do."

"I could tell."

"My problem is that *your* foot is in *my* way."

I stuck my tongue out at her.

The game continued with no more "incidents". In fact, everything went smoothly until it was time for cake and ice cream. Mrs Newton had fixed up the table in the dining room. Streamers criss-crossed the ceiling and a huge bunch of balloons was tied in the middle. The table was decorated in a teddy bear theme: teddy bear paper plates and paper cups, a tablecloth with teddy bears all over it, and even tiny teddies for party favours.

The children "oohed" and "aahed" as they came into the room, and Mrs Newton helped them find seats. "I want you girls to sit down, too," she told the members of the Babysitters Club. "Place yourselves strategically around the table so you can pass things and give the kids a hand if they need help."

After a little scuffle with Claudia, I sat down next to Jamie at one end. Kristy was sitting on one side, two places away from me. Stacey was across from her, and Claudia was sitting across from me, at the opposite end of the table.

"Mary Anne, how would you like to pour the punch you made?" asked Mrs Newton when we were settled. "Then I'll bring the cake in."

"Sure," I replied. She handed me the heavy pitcher full of red juice and I walked around the table with it, carefully filling each cup halfway. When I reached Kristy I filled her cup to the top – and kept on going.

145

"Hey, watch what you're doing!" she exclaimed.

I watched.

"It's – that stuff's getting in my lap!" She jumped up.

"Oh, *so* sorry. My mistake," I said.

"You bet it's your mistake! What's the big idea?"

"What's the big idea? What's the *big idea*? That's what you get when you step on my foot and don't answer my note."

"What note?"

"You know what note."

"I do not." Kristy sat down and began mopping up her lap with a paper napkin.

At that moment, Claudia appeared with another napkin. She wiped up some of the punch by Kristy's plate, then walked around the table and flung the wet napkin in Stacey's face.

"Hey!" Stacey was on her feet in a flash. She ran after Claudia and smushed the napkin in *her* face.

The dining room was in an uproar. "Mommy!" called Jamie. He looked as if he was about to cry.

Mrs Newton chose that very second to walk into the dining room with Jamie's birthday cake, five candles (four plus one to grow on) flickering cheerfully.

She came to a standstill before she reached the

table. "Girls, what is going *on*?" She looked around. The room had grown silent. The members of the Babysitters Club were gathered around Kristy, whose lap was stained with the red punch. I was holding the pitcher over the mess on the table, and Stacey was smushing the wet napkin in Claudia's face. A lone tear ran down Jamie's cheek.

Nobody knew what to say.

After a moment, I took the napkin away from Stacey and put it and a dry one over the spilled punch. "Just a little accident," I said to Mrs Newton. "I'm sorry. We're *all* sorry." I looked meaningfully at the other girls. "Kristy, why don't you go in the kitchen and get cleaned up." Kristy walked dazedly out of the dining room. "Come on," I said to Claudia and Stacey. "We're just going to help Kristy," I told Mrs Newton. "We'll be right back."

In the kitchen, the other girls stared at me.

"I don't care what any of you says or what any of you thinks," I told them boldly. "I am calling a meeting of the Babysitters Club for right after the party. *Be there,*" I added. Then I returned to the dining room to pass out the birthday cake.

Chapter 15

There was no more funny stuff during Jamie's party. The members of the Babysitters Club felt so guilty about almost ruining it that we bent over backwards being nice to Jamie and helpful to Mrs Newton. Then, the end of the party was so hectic, trying to sort out all the prizes and goody baskets and find everybody's coats, hats, mittens and boots, that by the time the guests were gone, Mrs Newton had forgotten about the trouble in the dining room and the argument over Lucy. At any rate, we hoped she had, since we didn't want her to think we were immature or irresponsible.

When Kristy, Claudia, Stacey and I left the Newtons', we stood around uncomfortably in their front yard.

"Where should we have the meeting?" I asked. "Claudia? Your room as usual?"

She shrugged. "I don't care."

"Fine. We'll go to the Kishis'," I said firmly.

Kristy raised her eyebrows slightly, but she didn't say anything.

Mimi greeted us as we trooped through Claudia's front door. "Girls!" she exclaimed. "It is lovely to see you again."

I knew she meant, It's lovely to see you *together* again.

"Hi, Mimi," I said, and gave her a hug. "Guess what – I've finished the scarf for my dad except for the fringe."

"That is wonderful, Mary Anne," Mimi replied warmly. "I'll be glad to help you with it."

"We're just going to have a quick club meeting," Claudia told her grandmother. "We'll be done soon."

"All right, my Claudia. That is fine."

We climbed the stairs, ran by Janine's room, and took seats in Claudia's room. Everyone looked at me.

I swallowed hard, feeling nervous. Then I remembered how I had taken charge when Jenny had got sick. I reminded myself that I'd made a new friend and had worked out some problems with my father.

I drew in a deep breath. "We've been mad at each other for weeks now," I said. "And it's time we stopped. We almost wrecked Jamie's party today. I felt horrible. I know you guys did, too."

They nodded, looking somewhat ashamed.

"So," I went on, "we either make up or break up. Break up the club, that is. Because we can't run it when we're mad at each other. And I don't know about you guys, but I don't want to break up the club. I had to work pretty hard just to be *in* it at first."

It was Stacey who spoke next. "I don't want the club to break up, either," she said softly. "You guys are my only friends here in Stoneybrook."

"Kristy?" I asked.

"I want to make up, I guess," she said. "But somebody owes me an apology. We all owe each other apologies."

"Who owes you one?" asked Claudia.

Kristy paused. "I can't remember!" she ex-claimed finally. "I don't remember exactly who I'm mad at or why!"

I started to giggle. "Neither do I," I said.

We all begin to laugh. Claudia laughed so hard she rolled off her bed.

"Just to make it official, though," I said, "why don't we apologize to each other. Right now. Ready? One, two, three—"

"I'm sorry!" the four of us shouted, still laughing.

Then I added, "I'm sorry I used to be such a coward and I would never stick my neck out or make decisions or take charge. And I'm sorry about Mimi, Claudia."

Kristy and Stacey exchanged puzzled looks, then shrugged their shoulders.

"That's OK. I'm the one who should be sorry about that," replied Claudia. "And I'm sorry I'm careless and forgetful. I'm trying to change."

Stacey cleared her throat. "I'm sorry I'm conceited about having lived in New York. I like Stoneybrook ten times better, and you guys are much nicer than most of my old so-called friends."

"Well," said Kristy, "believe me, this isn't easy to say, but I'm sorry I'm so bossy. I mean, I *am* the club president, but I don't need to take charge *all* the time. And with Mary Anne around, it looks like I won't be able to any more. What's happened to you, Mary Anne? You've *changed* since our fight."

I blushed. "A million things have happened," I said. "It's hard to explain."

"You're wearing your hair differently," Stacey pointed out. "You look very pretty."

"Thank you."

"So your dad finally gave in?" said Kristy, looking awed. "Amazing."

"Not without a fight," I added, "but we have an understanding now. By the way, I can stay out until ten o'clock on Fridays and Saturdays, and until nine-thirty on weeknights."

Kristy's mouth dropped open. "Gosh. . ."

Everyone began talking at once. While Claudia showed Stacey some new eyeshadow she'd bought, Kristy leaned over and said, "Mary Anne, there's something I don't understand. What was that note you were talking about at the party?"

"I left a note in your locker today. I decided our fight had gone on long enough, so I wrote a letter apologizing to you. I thought you'd at least say you'd got it."

"But I didn't," said Kristy. "My—"

"Oh, no!" I interrupted her. "I must have put it in the wrong locker!"

"No, you didn't. At least, I don't think so. What I'm trying to tell you is that my locker's broken. I couldn't get into it today. The janitor said he'd try to open it and put a new lock on it, but he probably won't be able to do that until tomorrow."

"Oh . . . Kristy, I'm sorry."

"So am I, but I think we've done enough apologizing today. Friends?"

"Friends."

She stuck out her hand and we shook on our friendship.

That evening I got home at 6:05 and heard the phone ringing. I unlocked the front door and barrelled through the hallway and into the kitchen. The phone had rung about six times and was still ringing. I snatched up the receiver.

"Hello?" I said breathlessly.

"Hi, it's me, Dawn. Oh, I was *hoping* you'd be there."

"What's up?"

"Mary Anne, you won't believe this. You know how disorganized my mom is? Well, she's still unpacking a few stray cartons, and she came to one labelled SPORTS EQUIPMENT, and guess what was inside."

"What?"

"A photo album. An old one. And guess what was inside that."

"What? *What?*"

"A *prom picture.*"

"*Aughh!* Was it my dad and your mom?"

"*Yes!* And my mom did have a rose pinned to her dress, and a white ribbon was tied to the stem. So I asked her who the guy was, and her voice got all soft and sort of dreamy, and she said, 'Oh, that was Richie Spier. . . I wonder whatever happened to him,' and I said, 'Nothing.' I mean, not *nothing*, Mary Anne, just that he hasn't gone anywhere. And she said, 'Nothing? How do you know?' and I said, 'Because he's Mary Anne's father. He's still right here in Stoneybrook.' And my mom nearly fainted!"

"Wow!" I exclaimed. "I wonder – just a second, Dawn. I think my – Dawn, Dad's home! I've got to ask him! I'm dying to! I'll call you back after dinner. Bye!"

With my father, you can't just jump into things. I didn't say a word about Dawn's mother until dinner had been made and we were sitting at the table eating.

I asked how his day was.

He asked how mine was.

I asked how his cases were going.

He asked how school and the Babysitters Club were going.

Then I said, "Dad? Did you ever know someone named Sharon Porter?"

Dad choked on a mouthful of carrots and had to drink some water before he could answer. "Sharon Porter? . . . Yes. Yes, I did. Why do you ask?"

"Well, I just found out that Dawn's mother was

Sharon Porter before she got married, and that she grew up in Stoneybrook. Dawn and I thought it would be really funny if you two knew each other in high school. . . Did you?"

"As a matter of fact, we did."

"Were you friends?"

Dad paused. "Yes," he said softly. "Very good friends. But we drifted apart. We didn't keep in touch. Her parents and I didn't get along very well. . . Sharon and I graduated from high school, we dated all that summer, and then we both went off to college. After college, Sharon moved to California. I lost track of her then. . . So Sharon got married?"

"And divorced," I pointed out. "She brought Dawn and her brother back here to Stoneybrook so they could all start over again. . . . How come you and the Porters didn't get along?"

"Oh, it's a long story. Let's just say that they didn't think I was good enough for their daughter. My family didn't have much money when I was growing up."

"Grandpa was . . . a mailman?" I asked, trying to remember. Dad's parents had died by the time I was in first grade.

"That's right. And Mr Porter was – is – a big banker."

"I wonder if you'd be good enough for Dawn's mother now," I mused.

A faint smile appeared on Dad's lips. "Don't go getting any ideas, Mary Anne," was all he would say.

When dinner was over, I asked, "Dad, could I use the phone . . . just for a few minutes? I don't have much homework."

"All right," he said vaguely.

I ran to the upstairs extension and dialled the Schafers'. "Dawn!" I cried. "I got the story. Or part of it anyway. Dad went all sort of dreamy, too. He's still dreamy." I told her what I had learned.

"Hmm," she said. "We'll have to do something about that."

"Yeah," I agreed. "Wow, it's been some day. I made up with Kristy, too. In fact, the whole club has made up."

"You have?" Dawn asked wistfully.

"Yup. Gosh, I wish you could belong to the Babysitters Club, too. You were great with Jenny last Saturday. Did you do much babysitting before you moved to Stoneybrook?"

"Tons," she replied.

The wheels began to turn in my head. "Listen,

Dawn, I have to go. I'll see you in school tomorrow, OK?"

"OK. See you."

"Bye." I hung up the phone. I hoped Dad would let me make one more call. I had something important to discuss with Kristy.

Chapter 16

My father has lost his mind. Honest. I can't believe what he said to me the other day. He said, "Yes." The amazing thing is that he said yes *after* I said, "Dad, may I have a Babysitters Club party at our house?"

So yesterday, Friday, I gave a special party. It was special because, aside from Kristy, Claudia and Stacey, there was one guest who wasn't a club member – yet. Dawn. I'd told the others all about her, and they wanted to meet her. They knew that I'd like her to become a club member. I wasn't sure how they'd feel about that. We'd had to look for new club members once before, and that was a disaster. But Dawn was different.

My party was held from five to eight. Dad and I ordered a large pizza, and my father even came home from work early to help me toss a salad. (We made a hamburger patty for Stacey, since she shouldn't eat pizza, because of her diabetes.)

At quarter to five, the doorbell rang.

"Yikes! It's starting," I said to Dad. "And they're early! Well, I think everything's ready." We were going to hold a getting-to-know-Dawn meeting in my room first, then eat in the kitchen (*with* Dad – he insisted), and then go back up to my room to fool around.

"Don't worry, your party will be fine, I'm sure," Dad told me. "You better go let your guests in," he added, as the doorbell rang a second time.

"OK," I replied, and it was then that I tripped over the empty pizza box (the pizza was warming in the oven), and fell against the kitchen counter, spilling a glass of diet soda and knocking a pile of carrot peelings to the floor.

"Oh, no!" I cried. My denim skirt was covered with soda.

"Relax, Mary Anne," said Dad calmly. "I'll get the door. You clean up."

I sighed. "All right. What a way to start a party."

Dad adjusted his glasses and headed for the front door. I got out the paper towels and started mopping up.

It took me a moment to realize that after I'd heard the door open, there had been absolute silence. I waited a few more moments, then peeped into the front hall.

What I saw nearly took my breath away. Dawn was in the hall, taking her coat off – and her mother and my father were standing at the door, staring at each other. Dawn saw me, grinned, and gave me the thumbs-up sign.

I opened my eyes wide. Then I grinned, too. Despite the fact that my hands were sticky and little pieces of carrot were clinging to my soda-soaked skirt, I joined the others in the hall.

"Dad," I said, "this is Mrs Schafer, Dawn's mother. Mrs Schafer, this is my dad, Mr Spier." I waited for a reaction. "I think you two know each other," I added.

My father recovered himself. "Yes. Yes, of course we do. Sharon, it's wonderful to see you. It's been years."

"It's good to see you, too, Richie," replied Dawn's mother.

Richie! I had to put my hand over my mouth to keep from giggling.

"Please come in," my father went on.

"Oh, I'd love to, but I can't stay," said Mrs Schafer. "I've got to pick up Dawn's brother at hockey practice."

"Dawn," I said quickly, "there's a huge mess in the kitchen. Come help me clean it up."

"Oh, sure," she replied. We hustled into the

kitchen. But we didn't clean up. We hovered by the door, trying to hear what was going on in the hall.

"I'm glad you're back in Stoneybrook," my father said. "Would you like to have dinner sometime?"

"I'd love to. When?" was the fast answer.

"When?" Dad repeated, sounding flustered. "Well, how about tomorrow night?"

"Wonderful."

"I'll see you tomorrow, then," said my father.

Dawn and I looked at each other. We gripped hands excitedly. A *date*! Our parents were going to go out on a *date*!

"Oh, and I'll drop Dawn off tonight," added Dad. "No need for you to make another trip."

Mrs Schafer thanked my father and left. Dad returned to the kitchen, looking dazed.

Dawn and I were pretty dazed ourselves. I thought I'd never be able to concentrate on the party after what had happened, but by the time the mess had been cleaned up, I'd changed my skirt, the members of the club had arrived, and we were sitting around in my room, I felt much calmer.

I'd introduced Dawn to the other girls as they'd arrived. Now Dawn and Kristy looked at each other warily.

"Mary Anne says you've done a lot of babysitting," Kristy said.

"Oh, yes," replied Dawn. "In California – that's where we used to live – I babysat all the time. We lived in this neighbourhood where there were tons of families and kids. I started sitting when I was nine. I bet I took care of every kid on my street at one time or another."

"Have you ever had an emergency?"

I could see that Kristy, as our president, was really going to grill Dawn. Then again, that was her job.

"An emergency?" said Dawn. "Well—"

"She was terrific when Jenny Prezzioso was sick," I interrupted. I had told the others about our hospital adventure.

Kristy nodded.

"And once," added Dawn, "there was a fire in a house when I sitting. It was a problem with the wiring. I got the kids outdoors and called the fire department."

"Wow," exclaimed Claudia, looking impressed. "Then what happened?"

"The firemen came really fast and put the fire out. The kitchen was all wet and smoky and black, but none of the other rooms were hurt."

"That was a pretty good emergency," said

Stacey, looking hopefully at Kristy.

I smiled at Stacey, saying a silent thank-you.

Kristy wasn't finished, though. "Have you ever taken care of a baby? I mean, a *real* baby – a newborn?"

Dawn paused. "No, not a newborn," she said slowly. "I think the youngest baby was Georgie Klein. He was about seven months."

"How late can you stay out?" (That was Kristy's favourite question.)

"Gosh, I'm not sure," said Dawn. "I'd have to check with my mother. Maybe ten o'clock? I don't know about school nights, though. It's been a while since I babysat for anyone besides my brother. The last kid I took care of was in California, since I don't know many people here. Mom's probably changed the rules since we moved."

Kristy looked satisfied.

"How come you moved, Dawn?" asked Stacey. "Did your father get transferred?"

Dawn glanced at me, then lowered her eyes. "Divorce," she replied.

"Your parents got divorced?" said Kristy. She sounded sympathetic. "Boy, I know all about that. Mine are divorced, too. It stinks."

"And I know all about moving," said Stacey. "My parents and I moved here from New York

163

last summer. That wasn't so great at first, but it's a lot better now."

"Yeah, that's because she met all these wonderful friends!" Claudia waved her hand around the room, indicating the club members.

"And now Dawn's meeting us," I said pointedly. I looked at Kristy and raised my eyebrows.

She smiled at me. "We sure have a lot of clients now, more than we know what to do with. We could use some help." She turned to Claudia and Stacey, who nodded their heads ever so slightly.

"Mary Anne?" said Kristy. "Do you want to say it?"

I grinned. "Sure. Dawn Schafer, would you like to join the Babysitters Club?"

The smile that spread across Dawn's face was one of the brightest I'd ever seen. "*Really?*" she cried. "I mean, yes! Yes, I want to join. More than anything! Thanks, you guys."

I jumped up. "Well," I said, "the pizza's warming up and I'm hungry. I think the Babysitters Club should go pig out."

Kristy, Stacey, Claudia, Dawn and I thundered down the stairs and into the kitchen. Kristy and Claudia attacked the pizza with our pizza cutter.

"Dad?" I called. "We're going to eat now!"

My father came into the kitchen. He looked as if he were moving underwater. Dawn and I glanced at each other. We both knew what my dad was thinking about, and we absolutely could not wait until Sunday morning to find out about our parents' date.

I was glad I had the Babysitters Club – the *five-member* Babysitters Club – to help keep my mind off of Saturday night.

I took a piece of pizza and held it in the air. "Pizza toast!" I cried. Kristy, Claudia, and Dawn raised their pizza, too, and Stacey raised her hamburger. (Dad didn't know *what* was going on.)

"To our new member," I said.

"To our new member," said Kristy, Stacey and Claudia.

"To *me!*" cried Dawn. "Thanks for letting me join the Babysitters Club."

Suzi had been helping Marnie build a tower of paper cups. She looked up with interest. "I wonder how long divorce lasts," she said.

"It's for ever," I replied, surprised.

"That's what Mommy said, but. . ."

"But you keep hoping your dad will come back?"

"Yeah," said Buddy and Suzi at the same time.

"Me, too," I said, "except I know he won't."

"Do you miss your dad?" asked Buddy.

"Very much."

"Me, too."

Buddy moved over until he was sitting next to me. I put my arm around him. Then I held my other arm out to Suzi, but instead of joining us, she jumped to her feet.

"You. Are. A. Liar!" she cried, pointing her finger at me. "A *liar*." Then she ran out of the playroom and upstairs.

"What did I say?" I asked Buddy.

Buddy frowned. "I think it was the part about daddies not coming back. She *really* thinks ours is going to come home for good one day."

"Hmm," I said. "Well, we'll leave her alone for a while."

Buddy turned on a cartoon show and settled down to watch. I decided to take Marnie upstairs to change her diaper. Marnie shared a room with Suzi, but Suzi wasn't in the room. The door to the bathroom was closed, however.

As I was finishing up with Marnie, the bathroom door opened a crack. Suzi peeked through. "Dawn?" she asked.

"Yeah?"

"I-I had an accident." Suzi scrunched up her face and began to cry.

"Hey, that's OK," I said. "Accidents happen." I put Marnie in her crib, and stepped into the bathroom, closing the door behind me.

"I wet my pants," Suzi moaned.

"It's really all right," I told her. I grabbed some paper towels and mopped up the puddle on the tile floor.

"Do we have to tell Mommy?" asked Suzi.

"Not if you don't want to. Here, we'll rinse out your trousers and your underwear, and get you some clean trousers. Then you'll be all set."

By the time Suzi and Marnie and I were on our way downstairs, Suzi was smiling again. A few minutes later, Mrs Barrett came home. I wish I'd had a camera so I could have recorded the look on her face when she saw the clean house.

"You're a wonder, Dawn!" she exclaimed.

"She's the best babysitter we ever had," said Buddy.

"She's our favourite," Suzi chimed in.

"I hope you'll come back," said Mrs Barrett as she paid me.

"Anytime," I told her cheerfully.

If I had only known then how often "anytime" was going to be, I might not have spoken so quickly.

Don't miss a meeting of

Read them all!